Noticing Paradise

Noticing
Paradise

ELLEN WITTLINGER

Houghton Mifflin Company
Boston   1995

Library of Congress Cataloging-in-Publication Data

Wittlinger, Ellen.
  Noticing paradise / Ellen Wittlinger.
     p.   cm.
  Summary: Sixteen-year-olds Noah, who is upset over his parents'
divorce, and Cat, who has always been sheltered by her parents, find
adventure and romance on a tour of the Galápagos Islands.
  ISBN 0-395-71646-2
  [1. Interpersonal relations — Fiction.   2. Galápagos Islands —
Fiction.]   I. Title.
PZ7.W78436No   1995   94-26410
[Fic] — dc20   CIP
                            AC

Printed in the United States of America
HAD 10 9 8 7 6 5 4 3 2 1

For David
who taught me to notice

and for Kate and Morgan
who do it so naturally

The islands of Casanova and Lorenzo are not real places; the story of the orphan tortoises is also fictitious. Four of the original fifteen subspecies of the Galápagos tortoise are now extinct. All other information about the biology and geology of the Galápagos Islands is as true as I know it to be, although distances between some localities may have been changed slightly to suit the story.

1/Noah

There I was in the middle of nowhere. Just me, my brother Henry, and two hundred international tourists looking stupid in a dozen different languages. All around me, happy campers in straw hats and sunglasses waited impatiently for their passports to be stamped so they could lug all that camera equipment and snorkeling gear on to the next phase of the adventure. All I could think of was, What am I doing here?

We'd spent the night in a luxury hotel in Quito, Ecuador — only the best when Dad's paying — which was indistinguishable from a big American hotel where you never actually have to see the people who live in the city you're visiting. In the morning we flew into Baltra, one of the many islands that make up a group called the Galápagos Islands, six hundred miles from mainland Ecuador and home to thousands of odd-looking birds you'd never see any place else on earth.

Whoopie. I mean, birds were not really my thing. But then, this trip had very little to do with me anyway. I just went along with the plan. I was compliant. I caused no trouble. I was sixteen years old and I didn't really give a damn what I did for the summer. Actually, I didn't give a damn about much of anything. I was floating.

Henry jabbed his elbow into my ribs, the jock method of getting someone's attention.

"Hey, there's one for you, Noah!" he said, nodding his head toward the little family group getting stamped through customs. Two nondescript gray-haired parents smiled at the inspector; each of them had a hand resting on the back of a short girl with shiny black hair, like they were afraid she'd float up into the air if they didn't hold her down.

"What are you talking about?" I asked Henry, though I knew all too well. Henry's conversational repertoire was limited to females and the wide world of sports, usually in that order. He had just graduated from college, where he double-majored in Skiing and Lifestyles of the Rich and Tanned.

"That girl. She looks about your age. She has potential," he said, sizing her up from behind.

The girl turned so I could see her face. Nothing extraordinary about it, except big eyes. "She looks about twelve. Besides I'm not interested in girls this summer."

"Right," he smirked. "You get dumped by some cute little cheerleader?"

"Henry, I never dated a cheerleader in my life. I got dumped by my cute little mother into the middle of the Pacific Ocean. With you."

"Hey, listen, your mom's not so bad. I always liked your mom."

"I know."

"At least she lets you sit on the furniture in your own house. Not like Clara the Cleaner. Besides, you shouldn't blame your mom for the divorce. It was Dad — he just can't stay married to one person," Henry explained as we gave our passports and a wad of money to the inspectors. "Your mom lasted longer than mine. And they both lasted longer than Evelyn."

There's something I haven't mentioned. Henry and I are half brothers. We have the same father, but different mothers. Dad was also married once before Henry's mom, but Evelyn had enough sense not to have any children so she's not part of our extended nuclear family. The only reason I know about her at all is because every Christmas she sends us a card with a photograph of her and her second husband and their five adorable blond children. This year's note mentioned the celebration of their twentieth wedding anniversary and their oldest daughter, the flute genius, going to Julliard.

Dad met Mom while he was still married to Clara. I know Mom always felt bad about that, like she was responsible for their divorce. I always thought her doting over Henry was guilt-induced.

Henry never seemed to hold anything against Mom. He always liked spending time at our house, though it never added up to more than a few weeks a year. Which is why I don't really know the guy all that well. When he was thirteen and I was seven Henry told me my mother was a babe, which I think probably scarred me for life.

And if that didn't do it, I figured this trip probably would. "I don't blame her for the divorce," I told him. "I blame her for lying to me. I blame her for pretending everything was great. No problem. Happy family. Then all of a sudden — bang, Dad's moved out, she doesn't want to talk about it, at least not to me, and I'm sent to Paradise Lost with you."

I did blame her for those things — it was true. And yet, if I was going to be the one to hand out the sentences of guilt, Dad would be the one locked up without bail.

Was it only six weeks ago that I was still a dumb, happy guy? I'd skipped baseball practice to study for a chemistry test, and come home from school early. I heard Mom and Dad talking in the kitchen. I stood outside the screen door and watched the whole thing, and all the time I kept thinking, This could never happen to *my* parents!

Mom sat on a stool at the kitchen counter while Dad paced a wide semicircle around her.

"You know as well as I do, this marriage is not what it once was," Dad explained patiently. "I don't think you love me anymore either."

"Don't tell me how I feel, Hank." Mom's jaw was clenched shut. I steadied myself on a lawn chair. Surely nothing bad could be happening here. We were a great family. Why we'd all taken the boat out together just last weekend!

"Look, Carol, you don't really *need* me anymore," Dad said.

Mom just sat staring at him. "What do you mean, I don't need you?" The skin that stretched over her "famous cheekbones," as Dad always called them, seemed suddenly puffy and soft.

Dad ran his hand through his hair and turned his back on her. "I mean, financially the gallery is in good shape. You have your reputation now. You're so busy I hardly see you anyway!"

"Hank, you're the one who's always gone! My need

4

for my husband is not merely financial!" The tears started to run from her eyes and I felt them on my own cheeks, too.

"Of course not. You know I didn't mean that, Carol." Dad walked over and put his hand on her shoulder, but she batted it away like it had stung her.

"It's always the younger woman who needs you most, isn't it, Hank? Why was I stupid enough to think I'd be any different from the others, once I got a few lines around my eyes, didn't look so stunning in a low-cut dress anymore?"

Every time Dad came near her, Mom moved away. I could tell she wasn't used to being this person, somebody people felt sorry for, somebody who wasn't getting all the breaks. She pulled herself back together then and threw my father out of the house.

After that her face seemed polished with hatred all the time. Even when she looked at me, the surface didn't crack. I felt like I was no longer just her son. Now I was also a *man*, the kind of person who could inflict this kind of pain on a woman.

I wanted to tell her, "It's not *my* fault. *I* still love you!" But I couldn't. I'd never said it to anyone before, not even her, and it seemed like I didn't even know the pronunciation of the words.

"Cheer up, Bud." Henry brought me back to the present. "Even if there aren't many girls on the boat, I've heard the snorkeling's great!"

Henry was so much like Dad it was spooky. Forget your troubles; come on, get happy — that's them. No problem is so great that a good game of tennis or squash can't put it in perspective. Or a new girlfriend.

Henry stuck our passports back in his beltpack and took off. "Come on. There's a sign for our boat!"

Standing just outside the minuscule airport were half a dozen young men and women holding signs with the names of ships on them. *Isabela. Fernandina. Encantada. M/V Santa Cruz.* The sign we were headed for, *M/V Santiago,* was being held in the air by a remarkable-looking woman, dressed all in khaki just like an American forest ranger, but with a swarm of dark brown curls reaching halfway down her back and bare, tanned feet that seemed perfectly at home walking back and forth on the rocky dirt.

Henry was smitten. But then Henry was smitten at least three times a day, so I didn't pay too much attention.

"*M/V Santiago?* Board this bus please," the woman announced in English thick with a rhythmic Spanish accent.

Henry was unable to walk past her. "You must be a guide on the boat," he said, flashing her his stun-gun grin.

"Yes, I am. If you're going to the *M/V Santiago,* please board the bus now."

I walked on, but Henry didn't follow. He stood there smiling. I had to admit, the smile seldom failed him.

"How long have you worked as a guide?" he asked.

"A long time." She turned away.

"Couldn't be *too* long. How old are you, maybe twenty-five?" He relaxed into his conversational stance, but only for a moment. The woman gave him a glare from hell.

"I don't believe my age should be important to you,

Sir. Which boat will you be sailing on?" She spit the words in his face.

Henry was shocked by his failure. "Um, this one. The *M/V Santiago.*"

"Then *please* board the bus, sir."

"Yes, ma'am!" Henry rallied and saluted her, even gave her a wink, but she wasn't looking anymore.

As we threw our bags down in the back of the bus, Henry muttered, "At least now we know what M/V stands for: Mostly Virgins."

I had to laugh a little, even though I couldn't help thinking Mom would hit the ceiling over a crack like that. "No, it probably means Mainly Vegetarians." Or, I thought to myself, maybe just Monotonous Voyage.

"More Vodka," Henry sang out, stretching his feet into the aisle and making himself comfortable. "My advice to you, Noah, is have fun. Hey — Dad's paying. If you don't like the wildlife, you can at least catch some rays. And I hear the food's good on these boats."

I looked out the window as the gassy old bus groaned across the dry island to the boat dock. Skinny cactus trees and some weedy-looking grass dotted the dry earth. A sliver of blue water was visible in the distance. It was hot, very hot, and the bus was kicking up clouds of dust that billowed through the half-open windows and clogged up my sinuses. I thought paradise had palm trees and waterfalls. Henry probably expected the women to be wearing bikinis and flower necklaces. Hawaii this was not.

I looked around at my fellow passengers, average ages forty to sixty, with the exception of a kid about eight screaming his head off about not getting a T-shirt from

7

the vendor at the airport. There was an elderly couple arguing about who had been carrying the raincoats when they got off the airplane, and a middle-aged woman was chattering away to anyone who'd listen about storms at sea. It seemed she'd never been on a boat that didn't manage to find one.

Great. Maybe I should have taken a motion-sickness pill after all. Not to counteract the rocking of the boat; it was dealing with all these strangers that would make the ride bumpy. I just felt like being alone for a while. And here I was, right in the middle of sixty people's fabulous vacation.

2/Cat

Okay — I admit the trip was not high on my list of ways to spend the money, but then I didn't win it. Mom did. I, Cat Mancini, could be on my way to Paris or Venice right this minute! Famous cities! Exotic people! Or we could have bought a computer — two computers! Or a horse, or a music system, or something exciting like that.

I should have known Mom and Dad would be more interested in exotic birds than exotic people. And purchasing tangible objects was always hard for them. Every year we put off getting a new couch in favor of a vacation, even though the blanket that covered the rips in the upholstery was getting pretty ripped itself. But the three of us had driven over most of the northwestern part of the United States and some of Canada, and I guess I'd have to agree with Mom — memories are worth more than furniture.

Actually the decision was a pretty democratic process. We all got to list the top five things we'd like to do with five thousand dollars. The problem was, Mom and Dad both had the same top thing on both their lists: a trip to the Galápagos Islands. Now I know all about the Galápagos; a girl can't grow up with a biologist for a father and not know about the Galápagos. They're famous. Charles Darwin based the whole origin of the species thing on research he did there. And it sounded like kind of a cool place to go, but not cooler than Paris.

I'm not complaining — I got my camera, too. Since the trip didn't cost the whole amount, Mom and Dad decided I could get the camera I'd been dreaming about — the one they couldn't afford to get me for my birthday — the Janus XR15 with three separate lenses. With this camera I could be happy vacationing in Siberia.

And Mom got the couch recovered, too. She said when you thought about it, what was the sense of buying a whole new couch?

Once we got off the plane on Baltra, it all started to seem pretty exciting. There were people speaking Spanish and English, French and German, even Japanese! Baltra itself was flat and dry, but there were these great gnarly cactus trees all over the place. I got out the Janus and started snapping away.

Mom and Dad were ecstatic. The first thing they saw when we walked out of the airport was a bunch of little Darwin's finches flying in and out of a bush. I thought they might start crying or something, so I got on the bus right away. But when we got off the bus, there were pelicans all over the place, swooping and nose-diving right in front of us, and I actually *did* see a little tear sneak down Mom's cheek. I didn't really blame her. Who could have imagined we'd ever be in a place like this, so far from home, with everything so different and amazing?

We took little rubber boats called pangas from the pier out to the deeper water where the *M/V Santiago* was docked. It was white and beautiful — bigger than I thought it would be, with a dining room and a bar and a store where you could buy all kinds of Ecuadorian crafts. And I had my own room! It was very small — all the rooms were — but at least I had a little privacy.

Best of all, once we got on the boat Mom and Dad entered their own private heaven and didn't seem to care that I wasn't on the same cloud. They were so excited they were practically hyperventilating. I took my book and went up on the top deck, leaving them alone to unpack and get ready for dinner. But how can you read when there's this incredible view all around? I almost went back to get my camera, but then I decided I ought to take it all in this way first, kind of soak it into my skin, before I relied too much on my eyes, or my "other eyes," as I sometimes thought of the camera. I could see three different islands from there, two low and flat, and one large, with a high peak. From the map I decided it must be Santa Cruz, a volcanic island. I was sitting here in the middle of volcanos!

There were big black birds flying overhead too, probably frigate birds. Dad would know for sure. And some kind of gulls that I didn't recognize. I sat there a long time, almost hypnotized by being in such a strange place, when suddenly I realized it was getting chilly; the sun was on the horizon and I was the only person still up on the deck.

Now this may not seem like a big thing, but believe me, it is without precedent in my life: Mom and Dad had actually gone in to the dining room and forgotten to come and get me! At home, dinnertime could be rearranged to all sorts of odd hours so that all three of us could sit down at the table together. It was one of Mom's Sacred Laws. So you can imagine my shock at finding they were so anxious to meet the other boat people, they forgot all about me.

Just walking on a boat took some getting used to. As I made my way down the stairs, I hung onto the railing so I wouldn't bang around from side to side. When you didn't have anything to hang onto, you couldn't help walking like a bad actor pretending to be drunk, reeling to the left and then back to the right. It would have been embarrassing except that everybody looked the same.

I bumped into Dad, literally, just as I got to the dining room. He was full of apologies, but I assured him I was proud of their new independence. They'd already chosen a large table, hoping lots of interesting people would join them, which seemed like a crapshoot to me. Wouldn't it be less risky to look around and decide who *you* want to sit with and then go and join *them?*

The three Japanese girls we saw at the airport were already sitting down talking to Mom. I knew she must be thrilled. For years she'd been wanting to have an exchange student live with us, but we didn't really have the room. She was a frustrated ambassador. Mom introduced me to Sachiko, who was apparently halfway through her life story.

"I been living in Quito one year," the tallest of the three said. "Tomoko also. But Miyoko come visit us summertime from Japan. Our good friend."

"I wanting learn more language," Miyoko explained. "All our Spanish good, but want English come better. We join English groupings for tour islands."

I was a little lost by this time, but Mom seemed to be following along perfectly well. "Oh yes, I saw your names on our list," she said. "We're all Albatrosses!"

It was an odd sensation to try to spoon up soup on a rocking boat. I kept watching the liquid slide gently to one side of the bowl and then the other. I had the feeling I might not find my mouth with the spoon. The whole process made me a little dizzy and I decided I better not think about it too much.

Then two more people came to the table, the two boys I noticed at the airport. One was older. I guess you couldn't really call him a boy. Both of them seemed older than me. They were handsome, but they obviously knew it. I had no interest in that kind of person. And, to be honest, that kind of person had never had any interest in me either.

"Hi! Mind if we join you?" the older one said. He had an enormous grin. Dad said by all means.

"My name's Henry Lowell," he announced and shook hands with my father before sitting down. The younger one had already plopped down, but then he shook hands too, sort of embarrassed. "My brother's Noah Barker-Lowell. He's my half brother, but he gets twice as many names!" Mom and Dad laughed politely, but I don't think they knew what he was talking about.

"Did I hear you say you're all Albatrosses?" Henry continued dominating the conversation. "So are we — isn't that a coincidence?"

I couldn't take it anymore. "What is an Albatross? I mean, I know it's a bird, but why are we them?"

Mom laid a hand on my arm. "I'll tell you in a minute, Catherine."

Captain Bolmeier was standing at his table in the front of the room and banging on a water glass with a spoon to get us all to shut up and listen to him. I didn't realize it then, but he was about to answer my question himself.

"Guten Abend! Buenas noches! Good evening!" he began. The poor man had to repeat everything he said three times in three different languages, so it took him forever to say anything. Meanwhile you had to look at this skinny old guy, about six and a half feet tall, dressed all in white with one of those captain's hats sitting at a cocky angle on his head. And he was wearing these tight white shorts with white knee socks that must have been specially made for him so they'd actually reach his knee, which was as high as the top of a normal person's thigh.

Anyway, the English explanation of how things worked was: the passengers were divided into four groups, Albatrosses, Boobies, Cormorants, and Dolphins. Cute, huh? These were some of the birds and animals we could expect to see in the next two weeks. The names were listed on the bulletin board, which is how everybody else already knew what they were. Albatrosses and Boobies were led by English-speaking guides, Cormorants by a German guide, and Dolphins by a Spanish guide. Each group had about fifteen members and went onshore together in its own panga.

Then the captain proceeded to introduce the guides. First was Annie, the Booby leader, an American girl with a big, broad smile, who actually waved to everybody like she was on a float or something. I thought I heard Henry snort and I turned around, ready to give the guy a nasty look when he made a crack about the Booby's boobs. Miraculously, he managed to keep his thoughts to himself.

Then came the leader of the Dolphins, Sofia, a beautiful Spanish woman I'd noticed at the airport. George was next, leader of the Cormorants, a German guy with bright red hair. Then the captain paused and smiled.

"And now I want to introduce you to the leader of the Albatrosses, Diego Alvarado." Everyone applauded politely, as we had for the others, but it was obvious the captain had more to say about Diego. For one thing, none of the other guides got to have a last name.

"The Albatrosses are fortunate to have a rather famous guide," Captain Bolmeier continued. Diego looked at his shiny white shoes. "I will let it be a surprise, but when you arrive at the Darwin Research Station on Santa Cruz Island, you will all see why we consider Diego something of a hero here in the Galápagos." The captain threw one arm around Diego's shoulders and smiled proudly down on him from above. Even the guides applauded him.

"Hey, we get the famous guide! Stick with me, guys — I'm always lucky," Henry announced, flashing a stunning grin around the table. I'd never met anybody with such a positive self-image. This Henry guy was slicing up his roast beef and flirting with Miyoko and complimenting my mother on her necklace all at the same time. His brother was not even on our planet, which, of course, made me wonder where he *was*. He stared at his dinner, picking apart the dilled potatoes, which I happened to think were quite tasty. I hadn't realized I was staring at *him* until he looked up at me and glared.

"And how old are you, Catherine?" Henry asked.

"I'm sixteen," I said. "People call me Cat."

"She just turned sixteen," Mom said, petting my shoulder in a very annoying way. "We still like the full name. She's named for her grandmother."

"Oh, I know the burden of family names!" Henry assured me. "I'm actually Henry Pinkham Lowell the Third! How'd you like to carry that title around?" He laughed and shook his head, obviously bursting with pride over his stupid name.

"Really?" Dad egged him on. "And what does your father do, Henry?"

"Ever heard of a company called Snowbird?"

"Oh, skiing equipment or something?" Mom said.

"Started as skiing, years ago. Now we do all kinds of outdoor equipment. Business is booming. Part of the reason I'm here is to test out some new snorkeling gear. Dad's considering buying the company. Cheaper in the long run."

"Well, isn't that interesting?" Dad lied. He had no interest in the world of business, and the only outdoor equipment he and Mom ever bought was binoculars. Two pairs. So as not to miss a bird while handing one pair back and forth.

After talking about himself for another fifteen minutes, old Henry got a clue. He turned to his brother. "Noah, you're quiet tonight. Noah is sixteen too, just like you, Cat. He gets to come along for the ride, doesn't even have to test out the equipment if he doesn't want to. We're bonding or something, aren't we, Bro?" Henry clamped a hand around Noah's shoulder and then let go, laughing loudly. The Japanese girls giggled.

Noah gripped his fork in his fist and for a minute I thought maybe he'd turn around and stick it in his brother's arm. I was hopeful. I caught his eyes for just a second and saw they were filled with anger, which made him seem more interesting than some regular handsome guy. But then he laid the fork down very quietly on his plate and didn't eat another bite.

Since Henry was quiet for half a minute, Dad decided to jump in and change the subject. "Well, I don't own any companies. I'm a biology teacher at our local high school and June teaches fourth grade. You'll never in a million years guess how we came to afford this trip."

Mom looked a little embarrassed. "Will, that may not interest —"

But Henry was eager to participate in the game. "Lemme guess. You got a reward for turning in a dangerous criminal? No? Oh, you won it somehow, is that it?"

"Yes, we did," Dad nodded. "But how?"

It was kind of a funny story, but it killed me how much Dad loved telling it.

"In the lottery? No. You wrote a poem about . . . No. Gee, some kind of a raffle or something?"

"You'll never guess it," I said. "Tell him."

"We won the money playing cow-plop bingo," Dad said proudly.

16

This made even Noah Barker-Lowell look up from the table. "What's that?"

"Oh, it's so silly," Mom said.

"It was a great idea!" Dad said. "Our local community center wanted to have a raffle to earn money for their renovations. So they divided the high school playing field into a grid — lines going both ways so the whole field was divided up into little boxes. Then everybody in town bought a box or two for twenty dollars each. The winner would get five thousand and the center would still make fifteen thousand for themselves. Everybody bought tickets."

"Then what?"

"Then they got a local farmer to come over with a cow one afternoon and they led the cow up and down the grid pattern, all over the field. And wherever the cow . . . plopped . . . that was the winner!"

Dad and Henry roared together. The Japanese girls were totally lost. The younger brother looked disgusted. I guess he was above discussing the bathroom habits of cows.

"Excuse me," he said, pushing back his chair. "I have a headache. Nice meeting you." He was in such a big hurry to get away he didn't even look at any of us. Interesting. There was something going on with that kid, and there was nothing I liked more than figuring people out.

"Not much of a conversationalist," Henry said, winking at Miyoko. "Any of you girls like to join me for a drink in the bar?"

"I will have Coke drink, Henry," Miyoko said sweetly. "Tamoko and Sachiko like drink orange soda."

Even though I was probably only a year or two younger than the Ko sisters, I was pretty sure this invitation didn't include me. Not that I had any interest in being part of a harem for some guy with four names who thought the world of himself. It just got me that I was still hanging around with my parents at my advanced age. Sometimes I felt like we were attached by bungie cords; I could only go so far before I'd have to come banging back into them.

"Well, I think I can arrange for a Coke and a couple of orange sodas," Henry smirked, herding his new girl-friends out of the dining room. He called back over his shoulder, "See all you Albatrosses tomorrow morning!"

Mom let out a deep breath. "Well, it's not like driving someplace by ourselves, is it?"

Dad put his arm around her shoulders, an unusual public display of affection. "June, this is the trip of a lifetime. Soak it all in!"

Mom smiled up at him as though they were alone at the table. Or maybe alone in the universe. Jeez.

Personally, I was looking forward to seeing what the Boobies had to offer. Could we change species? Maybe I could be a Dolphin and improve my Spanish. Maybe I could stay on deck and improve my tan. Two weeks suddenly seemed like a very long time.

3/Noah

Why did I ever go along with this plan? Dad kept billing it as a "trip to paradise" and "a chance for you to get to know your brother." At least Mom was more honest about it; she said it would do us good to be "out of each other's hair for a while." Me out of hers was more like it. She said my sulking and brooding was making her feel worse than she already did. Like her scowling at every male in sight was helping *my* depression.

I didn't even read any of the information about the trip. If I had I would have figured out I'd be stuffed in a tiny little cabin with Henry where there was only enough room for one of us to stand up at a time. The other person had to lie on his bed or hide in the bathroom. And there wasn't enough room to zip up your pants in the bathroom.

Of course most people didn't spend much time in their cabins. They went to the islands, they hung out in the dining room and the bar, they went to the gift shop, they slathered on an ounce of lotion and then baked their rear ends up on deck. One old guy already looked like grilled salmon. Not me. I intended to spend as much time as possible in my room, hibernating, until I could go home.

Thank god Henry immediately found females to hang around with. That got him off my back and out of the room. He stayed out half the night with his new friends. I felt kind of sorry for the Japanese girls, though. I didn't know if they'd ever run into anybody like Henry.

He was so thrilled when we walked into the dining room last night. "Look!" he said. "Your girl is sitting

19

with three for me!" He made a beeline for the empty chairs at their table. Sometimes I feel like *I'm* the college graduate.

It turned out the short girl with the black hair was my age. Close up she could pass for fourteen, I guess, but she's very unsophisticated. She kept staring holes through me but didn't say much. And her parents are bizarre. They told some long story about winning money betting on cow poop. Talk about hicks.

I could tell she was knocked out by Henry the Hunk. Henry said he invited all the girls to the bar with him after dinner, but this Cat was too shy to go. He thought this made her perfect for me. I'm not shy, I told him, I'm morose.

Anyway, I wasn't planning on getting up at dawn and going to an island, but they blared this loud music into all the cabins at 6:30 and then the captain came on yelling, "Guten Morgen! Buenos días! Good morning!" You'd have to be dead to sleep through it. I decided I'd have breakfast and see how I felt.

I purposely chose a tableful of Germans, figuring at least I wouldn't have to talk. But of course they wanted to be friendly and they knew practically as much English as I did, so they asked me about thirty or forty questions. I just wasn't in the mood for it. I finished my cereal and got a cup of coffee to take up on deck.

Turned out it was kind of nice up on deck. Since everybody else was eating, I was finally alone and I could kind of enjoy the place for a minute. The water was a deep, sparkling blue. If I'd been having a good time I'd have said it was beautiful. We were anchored not far from a small island which looked hot and rocky and not one bit like paradise. I figured it must be North Seymour since that was the island scheduled on the day's itinerary. Even from the *Santiago* I could see a lot of birds circling over the island, large black birds swooping and diving. Standing there looking around, I decided what the heck? I might as well go. There wasn't anything to do on the boat and I wasn't tired enough to go back to sleep.

"There's my man!"

There was no escaping Henry. He climbed up the stairs, followed by the Japanese girls. I swear, he's never in a bad mood.

"Come on! The groups are forming and the Albatrosses go first!"

I gave up and followed his entourage back downstairs.

"It's a dry landing, so you're okay in your sneakers," he assured me.

"What's a dry landing?"

"Noah, get with the program. Dry landing means you get out on land or rocks. Wet landing, you jump out of the panga in the water."

Already Henry was using these words like he'd known them since birth. Downstairs people milled around nervously, wearing backpacks and carrying camera bags. I realized I was the only person there without a hat or sunglasses, but it seemed too difficult to go down to the cabin and retrieve them. I wondered why all these people went to so much trouble and expense to do this. Wouldn't they rather be home in bed?

"There's Diego, our guide," Henry said. "I met him last night in the bar."

No doubt Henry was on a first-name basis with everybody on the boat by now. Diego was an intense-looking guy, dark-skinned and probably Ecuadorian, some kind of local legend or something. He probably invented some method for washing dried bird guano out of those snazzy white uniforms.

The captain called for all the Albatrosses to line up along the side of the boat, and everybody did as they were told. I felt like a second-grader being assigned to a reading group.

As we approached the stairs that went down the side of the boat, we were each handed a life vest of appropriate size. There were people all along the way to help you so you didn't slip and end up as shark food. Finally you made a little leap into the rubber panga and took a seat along the inflated edge.

I looked around at my fellow Albatrosses: Besides me and Henry and the Japanese girls, there was a middle-aged couple with a little boy — oh God, it was the brat from the bus, wouldn't you know — and two old codgers wearing big floppy rain hats. Then there was a younger couple who didn't seem to be speaking to each other. They were probably on their honeymoon. The last people to get on were our dinner companions, that girl Cat and her parents, looking a little frazzled. That was it — the people I'd be imprisoned with for the next two weeks. A stunning cast.

"The island we're visiting today, North Seymour, was formed by an uplifting of the earth on the bottom of the ocean." Diego was beginning to lecture. I didn't mind walking around looking at stuff, but did I have to listen to a geological treatise on everything? "The Galápagos are volcanic islands, many of them made up of material from lava flows. Only a few islands are like this one, lifted from the bottom of the sea to become dry land."

People were already oohing and aahing. When he got started on vegetation I decided to just keep my eyes on where we were going. Which is why I was the first one to spot it.

"A seal!" I yelled. I couldn't believe I yelled it out like that.

"Yes, a sea lion," Diego corrected me gently. He had a pleasant accent which softened the edges of his English. "Just at the spot where we'll be jumping out onto the rocks, so watch your footing, please, as well as the sea lion." The boat pulled up close and the sea lion didn't move a muscle.

"Aren't they afraid of the boats?" the elderly woman asked.

"You will notice that the animals and birds of the Galápagos have no fear of humans. Please be careful as we go along not to step on them or harm them. I remind you once more before we leave the boat: Take nothing from the island, not a shell or a feather or a rock. The ecosystems of these islands are very delicate and we must not disturb them."

Diego made eye contact with each of us, one by one, making sure we took him seriously. "Leave nothing behind on the island, no food or paper or trash. We return to the boat for lunch; no food should ever be taken to an uninhabited island. Do not touch any of the animals or birds, even though they appear to be tame. Your scent left on a baby sea lion will confuse the mother and she may not recognize the pup as her own. Over the last few centuries man has brought destruction to these beautiful islands. Now we are in the process of bringing paradise back."

The folks were practically in tears following that ecology report. As though we hadn't already seen all these same rules posted every five feet since we got off the plane at Baltra.

Diego and the panga driver helped us out onto the rocks. Sure enough, we walked about a foot away from the sea lion and it didn't even roll over. I was about to wonder if it was dead when I looked up and noticed about a dozen more lying strewn around the sand that topped the rocks.

There were lots of silky, brown babies, many of them nuzzling or nursing at their mothers. One mother came slapping across the rocks, barking loudly, when the group came between her and her baby. It was pretty amazing how fast they could move on those funny flippers. It looked sort of like they were running on their ankles with their feet flapping out to the side.

All around me the cameras were clicking and the camcorders were buzzing. The woman from the honeymoon couple kept saying, "I'dn that *cute?*" while her husband videotaped everything in sight. Even the brat was in awe. His mother took a picture of him sitting in the sand looking a sea lion pup right in the eye. It was hard to be immune, but I worked at it. I was glad I didn't have a camera.

The group forged on ahead, Diego pointing out land iguanas, lava lizards, and then — blue-footed boobies. I had to admit, I'd never seen anything so bizarre so close up for such a long time. The boobies were everywhere you looked — right under your feet, dancing around together, sitting on nests of eggs, hiding their scruffy white babies under their wings.

Their blue feet were like big flat paddles, and they picked them up high and perpendicular to the ground when they walked, like they were waving to one another. The group fanned out at that point, some listening to Diego go on about this or that, some taking pictures of each other with every living creature in the place. I decided I'd just sit down a minute and watch two boobies who were dancing around each other. It was a riot.

One of them fanned his wings out to about four feet and let out a piercing whistle, all the while showing off his ridiculous feet to the other one. The second one squawked like a turkey and kept hopping up and down on a rock. Then they'd stop and pass a stick back and forth. Then the whistling and squawking started again. I was kind of hypnotized by the whole thing.

"You like birds?" The blunt, questioning voice made me jump. I didn't realize there was anybody near me. But when I turned around I could hardly tell who it was. Somebody in jeans and a T-shirt was lying on her side in the sand, squinting into a camera with an enormous lens attached. Pretty black hair. It had to be Cat. She put a hand up to stop me from answering her question. Obviously she was in the middle of taking a Pulitzer Prize–winning booby photograph.

She clicked a few times, then sat up. "Sorry. I was seeing some great pictures and I didn't want to lose them."

I nodded. "Probably your last chance to see a blue-footed booby. Unless you walk five feet in any direction."

"You never know which picture will be the great one," she said, taking one roll of film out of her camera and loading in another. "So, you're into birds?"

I snorted. "Hardly. I mean these guys are pretty funny, but normally I can't tell a robin from a blue jay."

"And you're proud of that?"

"I didn't say I was . . ."

"These are not both *guys,* by the way. The male is the whistler, the one with the small pupil in his eye. The female has a larger pupil and makes the squawking sound. They're mating. This ritual can last a long time, passing the sticks back and forth, showing off their feet and their wing span."

"How do you know?"

"Diego just told us. I *knew* you weren't listening."

"Oh." I looked at the boobies again. "How can you tell how big their pupils are? I can't tell."

"I birdwatch with my parents sometimes. You get to notice things. I'd rather take photographs, though."

"That's a fancy camera," I said.

Diego was calling the stragglers to catch up, so we started to follow the path between booby nests, trying not to step on any that were in our way, which most of them were.

"I just got it," Cat said, "With cow poop loot. I've never had a good camera before. It's even more exciting than I thought it would be."

A camera was exciting? She'd be a barrel of fun.

"Where are you from?" I asked her.

"Oregon. A little town called Benson River. It's in the valley between the Cascades and the Siskiyou Mountains," she said proudly. Like I had any idea where that might be. "Where are you from?"

"I'm from Brookline," I said.

"Brooklyn? Really? I'd like to visit New York sometime."

"Not Brooklyn. *Brookline.* In Massachusetts. Just outside Boston, you know?"

She looked blank. "Never heard of it."

"You've never heard of Brookline? John F. Kennedy was born there. Michael Dukakis lives there!"

"You ever hear of Benson River before? Humphrey Wells lives there."

"Of course I never heard of Benson River. It's a little town way across the whole country. I've never heard of Humphrey Wells either."

"National champion bull rider six years running."

Was she putting me on here? I couldn't tell if she was smiling or not with that camera pressed up to her face all the time.

"Frigate birds!" she cried, slapping me hard in the chest in her excitement. Diego was already talking by the time we reached the group.

I was standing next to the guy who hadn't put his video camcorder down for one minute since we hit land. It was cracking me up. Diego would say something and then this guy would try to repeat the gist of it for his own video, except he was messing the whole thing up.

"This is the largest frigate nesting area you will see on the islands," Diego said.

"This is where the big black birds nest. We won't see any bigger ones on this trip," the guy tells the folks back home.

"Notice how the male blows up the red pouch under his neck, then puts his head back so the pouch is shown off to the sky. This is because the female, as she flies overhead, chooses a male by the pouch she likes best."

"So the male bird makes his neck big so the females can see it when they fly over. Or, I think maybe they make it red." Get a clue, fella.

"It's all up to the female. The male has no say in the matter." Diego looked around and smiled, ready to be personable. "Just like with humans. Yes?"

Most people laughed appreciatively. Ha, ha. What a funny guy. Even Cat was smiling at him idiotically. Personally, I didn't see that there was much similarity between birds that chose each other on the basis of neck size after half a dozen flybys and humans, who spent years trying to attract the perfect mate, then threw them over when somebody more perfect came along.

Henry didn't subscribe to the theory either. He was having his picture taken first with Miyoko, then with Sachiko, then Tomoko. Finally one of the girls asked Cat's mother to take a picture of all four of them together. I wondered if Henry would go down in Japanese history.

"So why *are* you here?" Cat had sneaked up on me as we followed the trail past the preening frigates. "I mean, it's a lot of money to waste on somebody who doesn't want to be here."

"You think I don't want to be here?"

"Doesn't take a genius. Half the time you're bored. Half the time you're mad."

Gee, don't beat around the bush. "I'm not mad now. I like this island."

"Pin a medal on you. You'd like it even more if you

listened to what Diego said instead of trailing way behind." She dropped to her knees and focused on a small
green lizard scuttling over a rock. "You missed his talk
on Darwin and the origin of the species. But I guess
everybody knows that stuff."

"Yeah." It sounded vaguely familiar.

"You *do* know about Darwin? Or don't they teach biology in Brookline?"

"Of course they do. I learned it, once. I couldn't explain it to you this minute. What's it got to do with the
Galápagos anyway?"

She laughed. "You must be the first person to ever
come on this trip without knowing what Darwin had to
do with the Galápagos."

What a pain in the neck this girl was. "Look, I don't
even care, okay?"

"You've heard of the survival of the fittest?" School
was still in session.

"Yeah, as a matter of fact, I have. That's when the
weak or sick animals are the ones who get caught."

"Correct! You go on to the Final Jeopardy round! Also,
the strongest animals are the ones more likely to live on
and mate, so their babies are more likely to be strong
too," she continued.

"As I recall this does not happen only in the
Galápagos."

She sighed, as though I was forcing her to lecture me.
"Of course not, but this happens to be the place Darwin
first noticed it."

"So? Where did that apple fall on Newton's head? Do
busloads of tourists stand around gawking at the tree?"

She glared at me. "Are you trying to be dumb?"

"It's not all that hard," I assured her.

"These very animals were the ones that helped Darwin figure it out!" she yelled at me.

"My, aren't they a talented lot," I said.

"These islands are so close together they're like a perfect laboratory." And she was like a Timex watch; once she started ticking, you couldn't turn her off. "The animals that survived were able to adapt to the environment. For instance, on one island the finches might have stronger beaks because there are only seeds to eat, but on another island they might have skinny beaks to dig up worms, but basically they're the same bird."

"You got all that from Diego?"

"No. My dad's a biologist."

"You didn't tell me you had an unfair advantage," I said, smiling a little.

"I'm sure you've had plenty of advantages of your own," she said right back. Jeez, did she always have to have the last word?

"So all Darwin did was open his eyes and notice it? For this he goes down in history?"

"I don't think noticing what's around you is a common human trait, Noah."

"I guess not. We haven't evolved all that far, have we?"

For the first time, Cat smiled. She had a big full smile that seemed to mean what it said. "So, how come you were so mad last night at dinner?"

"What are you, a detective?"

"I like to figure out what's going on with people." The terrain had gotten rougher. Cat hopped from rock to rock ahead of me.

"That could be called nosy."

"It could be called 'noticing.' "

"Okay. I guess I was mad last night. I didn't want to come here, but now that I'm here, I might as well make the best of it."

Cat turned and stared at me. "God! This is the dream vacation of a lifetime for most of these people and you're willing to put up with it!"

"You asked me and I told you." What was her problem?

"So, you're rich, I guess. That company your dad owns, Snowbees or something . . ."

"Snowbird. Look, I don't want to talk about my parents, all right?" I was tired of being interrogated. "Why don't you go take some more pictures?"

She planted herself in my path with a scowl on her face. "Don't you dare order me around! Who do you think you are?" Then she turned and stomped away. In a few seconds she came back. "By the way, you're a fool to be out in this sun without a hat on. Wait and see." That was the end of her sermon for the day.

Wouldn't you know Henry would be hanging around nearby. "Have a spat with Cat?" He thought that was hysterical.

"I only talked to her for a minute."

"Got under her skin though, didn't you? We Lowell men have a way of doing that."

Sometimes I just feel like punching Henry in the mouth. "God, Henry, I'm not a Lowell man, whatever that is. Who'd want to be? If Dad's such a great guy, why does he keep picking up and leaving his family behind?" Now I *was* mad and I hadn't even seen it coming.

"Hey, I'm not saying he's a saint. He just does what he has to do. He's a modern man, Noah."

"Bull. Why did he have to leave my mother?"

Henry gave me a long look. "Same reason he had to leave my mother."

"Why? Because his new girlfriend is younger or prettier?"

"No. Because his new girlfriend is pregnant."

4/Cat

I couldn't get over that Noah kid. He could be on some crowded beach in Florida for all he cared. He was sleepwalking through the whole trip. First he yelled at me to leave him alone, when all I was doing was making conversation. Then I saw him screaming at his older brother, who's a rather annoying dude himself. I figured the heck with both of them.

But then later he was sitting by himself on a rock, holding up his head with one hand, staring at the boobies again. He seemed kind of obsessed with the boobies.

"Got a headache, don't you?" I said. "Wear a hat next time."

"I will," he said. I started to walk past him, but then he said, "God, these are stupid-looking birds."

They are, but I didn't feel like agreeing with him. "You just think that because they're trusting enough to walk right up to you and let you laugh in their faces."

"Why *do* they trust people?"

Interesting question. "Well, they probably didn't see many people until the tour boats started coming around. And that's only gotten to be a big business the last decade or so."

"You'd think a decade would be long enough to figure out humans are not to be trusted."

I had a feeling we weren't talking about birds anymore. Something was obviously going on with this kid, but he wasn't about to tell me.

"The boobies remind me of stand-up comics," I said. "This whole island is like housing for retired comedians."

"They remind me of Rilke," he said after a minute.

"Rilke? What's that?"

"Rilke. The German poet. You never heard of Rilke?" He looked amazed.

"No, I never heard of Rilke! You are such a snob! Just because I don't happen to live on the East Coast and . . ."

He held up his hands to stop me. "Okay, okay! I guess there's no reason you should. I took an advanced English course last year and we studied Rilke. My mother named her Chihuahua after him. His eyes are beady and vacant just like these birds."

"The poet has beady eyes, or the dog?" I asked, smoothing my feathers a little bit. "I can't imagine somebody naming a dog after a German poet."

"She likes poetry. My mother, not the dog. We used to have goldfish named Whitman and Longfellow."

"I bet she's a librarian or something. Or owns a bookstore." I was imagining what she'd look like — a sweet smile and hair turning gradually white.

"No. She owns an art gallery on Newbury Street in Boston. It's a very ritzy area with lots of galleries."

"It's not one of those places where you have to ring a bell before they let you in, is it? I saw some places like that in San Francisco once. They gave me the creeps."

"Yeah, you ring a bell and then they let you in."

Goodbye to the kindly white-haired lady. "But if they were planning to just let everybody come in, they'd leave the door open, wouldn't they? So that means there are some people they *wouldn't* let in? I didn't want to ring the bell and find out!" I wasn't even sure if I wanted to be somebody they *would* let in or somebody they *wouldn't!*

"They'd let you in," he said, like he knew all about it.

"Well then, who don't they let in?"

"I don't know! You sure can twist a conversation into knots."

Diego was calling us to come and get in the panga to go back to the boat, so I left Noah and his headache behind. I couldn't figure out how to talk to the guy.

Not that I'm so great at talking to anybody else. My friends are constantly telling me to calm down or mind my own business. But I can never seem to figure out what's my own business and what's not. I hate for people to keep secrets. When a friend of mine has a secret I feel like you do when you've almost finished a big puzzle, but there's one piece missing. I go crazy until I've found that piece.

Maybe I should live in France. I was sitting up on deck reading a mystery in the afternoon and there was this French woman in the deck chair next to me. I was feeling blissfully alone — Mom and Dad were taking a panga ride around to the other side of North Seymour with a bunch of other people who couldn't get enough bird life — when suddenly this woman tapped me on the arm.

"Do you like mysteries?" she whispered. I nodded. "Look over there and tell me what is going on with those two."

She was pointing at the young couple from the Albatross group, the ones I thought might be on their honeymoon. They were standing at the railing and trying to keep their argument quiet enough so no one else could hear.

"A lovers' spat," the woman said, smiling. "Or perhaps they are not what they seem to be."

"I though they might be newlyweds," I said. "But do newlyweds argue?"

"They do," the woman said. "Perhaps we are seeing a sad unfolding of a story."

"Like what?"

We both stared at them for a minute. "Oh, probably it isn't serious. A quarrel of lovers. It will be over by the time the moon comes out." I loved listening to this woman talk; it was like quiet music.

I shook my head. "What I think is they're brother and sister and they came here to plot the murder of their uncle in order to avenge the death of their father. The thing is, she wants to hire the Terminator to do it, but her brother thinks it would be more fun to do it himself."

35

The woman shrieked with laughter. "Oh, you are better at this game than I am. Such an imagination!"

"Thanks. I'm older than I look. Where are you from?"

"Paris. My name is Monique LeFarge. I'm traveling with my sister. And you?"

"I'm Cat Mancini from Oregon, U.S.A.," I said. "I'm with my parents and I wish we'd gone to Paris instead of here."

Monique laughed. "Paris will be around a long time. Maybe you'll come visit me there sometime and we can make up stories about all the people in Montmartre."

I knew she was just being nice, but the idea of being able to visit an actual Parisian in Paris put me into daydream overdrive. "Over there!" I pointed to an old couple smearing suntan lotion on each other. "Very sad story. The husband has an incurable disease. Upon his death, the woman will inherit a large sum of money. Her love for him has waned in the past few years, and his long illness is eating up the money. It has occurred to her that an accident could befall him sometime during this trip . . ."

"Oh my, Cat! Let's hope not!" She had a tinkly laugh. "I prefer my stories to revolve around love. Especially love spurned, unrequited. The bittersweet love of hopelessness." She pursed her purplish mouth and stared out at the blue sea.

I'd never heard an adult talk like this. "Are you an actress?" I asked.

"No. I'm an architect. Why do you ask?"

"Just the way you talk."

She leaned in close to me. "Are you in love, little Cat?"

I hated for people to call me "little." After sixteen long years I'd finally managed to hit five feet, two inches and actually have some *use* for a bra, and I felt it should be noted. I made a face. "No, I don't find boys all that fascinating."

Well, okay, that was an outright lie. But I didn't feel like telling her that "little Cat" not only wasn't in love but couldn't even find a boy who thought of her as more than a kind of mascot. Little Cat had never even been on a real date!

My name, it turns out, is perfect. I'm a small creature with a big mouth who people pat on the head. But you'll notice the cat never gets to ride along in the car.

Monique laughed. "Very soon I think you will find boys very fascinating. Love is sweeter when you are sixteen than ever again."

Jeez, I was getting tired of listening to her expertise on love.

She stood up. "I should go and check on my sister, darling. She wasn't feeling too well. We'll talk more later." She smiled sweetly and disappeared below deck. I figured Monique was probably *poisoning* her sister, or else her sister was dying of bittersweet love.

By dinnertime I was tired of reading and ready to meet some more traveling cuckoos — this ship was obviously loaded with them. Luck was with me. Diego sat at our table. Diego might not have been as odd as some of the others I'd met, but he certainly got more gorgeous every time I looked at him. He had these deep, dark eyes you could pour out your soul to. Of course, I'd be willing to pour out my soul to somebody with light, shallow eyes too, but that's not the point.

I was also dying to know what made him so famous. Maybe I'd be able to get it out of him.

It must have been part of the job description for the guides to eat with the passengers at dinner, but I allowed myself the fantasy that he'd scanned the room and decided he'd rather sit next to me than anybody else.

I looked around to see where the other guides had settled for the meal. Annie was sitting with a tableful of middle-aged Boobies. Great howls of laughter kept bursting from their table. George, the German guide, was deep in conversation with people from his group.

At first I couldn't find the fourth guide, but then I turned around to see what the disturbance was in back of us. Sofia, the Ecuadorian guide for the Dolphins, was squaring off with old Henry the Third. He seemed to be blocking her path.

"Mr. Lowell, it is customary for the guides to dine with members of their own group. If you'll excuse me . . ." She pushed past him, but he stayed alongside her.

"Well, hey, I can eat with Dolphins, can't I? No rules about where the passengers eat, is there?"

She sighed. "No, of course not. You may eat wherever you like." She walked regally off to join a Spanish-speaking table and Henry plodded after her.

I couldn't help but laugh. "Look, she's got her own private Albatross — hanging around her neck."

"Catherine. Henry is just being friendly," Mom said, eyeing Diego. She doesn't mind me being cheeky if it's just our family, but it tends to embarrass her in front of strangers.

Diego smiled. "Don't worry about Sofia. She knows

how to discourage ardent passengers. It does happen once in a while."

"What if they get too ardent?" I asked.

"She's a black belt in karate," Diego said. "Nobody gets the best of Sofia." He looked over at her with what might have been affection, but since I preferred to hold on to my own fantasies about Diego, I decided it was merely respect. Yes, Sofia was nice-looking, you could even say she was beautiful, but probably she didn't appear so exotic to Diego. Whereas someone with pale skin and an American twang might be just what he wanted.

"What happened to Henry's brother?" Dad wondered.

"Probably in his cabin with a pounding headache," I said. "Dumb kid didn't wear a hat this morning. I told him he'd be sorry."

"Yes, that is most important in the tropical sun. Especially those of you with such light skin — I hope you are putting a good sunscreen on each day." Diego's dark eyes burned into mine. Just as I thought!

"Absolutely! I bought twenty-five SPF just for the trip," I assured him.

He smiled at me, but I must say he seemed a little distracted. He worked away at his food and made small talk with Dad, but the insights into life as a guide were not forthcoming.

"How long have you been a guide on the boat?" I asked him.

"Three years now."

"Do you like going to the islands every day?"

"Yes, of course I do," he said. "But before I worked on the boat, I worked at the Charles Darwin Research Station on the island of Santa Cruz. That I loved."

"What did you do there?" Now we were getting to it — the secret of Diego's fame.

"I helped in the breeding of the Galápagos tortoises. It was very enjoyable work." He pushed his food away as though it suddenly tasted bad.

"Why did you want to work on the boat then, if you liked breeding the tortoises?" Mom gave me a look that said I was getting dangerously close to nosy here, but I wanted to know.

He smiled. "Well, of course, working on the boat is enjoyable too. Here I get to meet people from all over the world. It can be very interesting." He stared off into the distance.

I could see he wasn't going to give me a straight answer. I mean, working on the boat might be okay for a summer or something, but for three years? Meeting a whole new group of people every two weeks, repeating the same information over and over, making sure they didn't steal feathers and step on sea lions. Breeding endangered tortoises sounded a lot more interesting to me.

Just then the laughter from the Booby table erupted loudly. Annie yelled, "One, two, three!" To the tune of "You Are My Sunshine," the entire table sang.

> *We are the Boobies, the only Boobies!*
> *We ride the pangas night and day.*
> *From Floreana to Santa Cruz-y*
> *You'll be sorry when the Boobies go away!*

Raucous laughter and applause erupted throughout the dining room. I turned to Diego to suggest the Albatrosses enter the song competition, but when I saw the sad expression on his face, I changed my mind.

"Annie is new on the boat," he said. "Still so much enthusiasm. It is nice for them." Then he rose and walked quietly away.

5/Noah

At first I wanted to kill Henry for telling me. But once I thought about it, I had to thank him. I mean, obviously people have been keeping secrets from me all my life. It's about time somebody started telling me the truth.

Dad married Mom because she was pregnant — with me. He left Clara and Henry behind and started a new family. Oh, sure, he always sent them plenty of money and Henry came to visit and everything. But I always knew I was Dad's *real* son. I was the one he lived with; Henry was just part of an early mistake Dad had made, before his real life began.

Only now he was starting another new life and Mom and I wouldn't be a part of that one. There would be another child who thought he or she was part of the real family, that I was the mistake.

Henry came back to the cabin after dinner last night. I'd gone to bed with a headache, but I couldn't sleep. He'd had dinner with that beautiful guide, Sofia, but apparently she wouldn't give him the time of day. And he was worried that the Japanese girls were getting too possessive of him, especially Miyoko (whose fault was that?), so he went to bed early too.

We lay there awake in the dark for quite a while. It felt to me like there were sparks of tension in the air.

"I thought you liked Miyoko," I said, just to say something.

"I do. She's fun and she's pretty. She's even smart, which I don't *require* from girls, but it's a pleasant change."

"Why would you waste your time on somebody who *wasn't* smart?"

"Noah, I don't have a consuming need to discuss world events with every girl I go out with."

"Maybe you ought to," I said, cranky as hell.

"Look, you're not upset about my dating habits. Just spit it out."

What I *was* mad about had burned a sore spot inside me that I wasn't anxious to touch. But finally I said, "How come you didn't hate me?"

He laughed. "Are you kidding? I was thrilled to have a brother. I'd been begging Clara to get me one, but she explained in graphic detail why she never intended to go through that again. I was a little upset though when I realized I wouldn't get to hang out with you much. Or with Dad."

"Yeah. I'm sorry."

"Hey, Bud, I never blamed anything on you. How was it your fault?"

"I don't know, but I think I might hate this new baby. I'm not as easygoing as you. Or not as nice a person."

"Nah. You were probably closer to Dad is all. He was

42

gone by the time I was five. Not much day-to-day stuff after that. You'll miss him more than I did."

For the first time since I'd heard about the divorce, I felt like crying. My chin started to shake and my throat burned. The tears piled up behind my eyes and finally I had to let a few leak out. But I didn't want Henry to know.

When I felt like I could talk again, I said, "Henry, I don't want to be like Dad."

He was almost falling asleep, but he rallied a minute. "I know, but the thing is, there are so many women. How can there only be one right one?"

I thought about that. "Maybe there isn't only one right one. Maybe there are a hundred people who would be right for you. Or a thousand. But you can't just keep marrying everybody, one after the other. You just decide, this is the person I'm going to stay with. I'll make it a good marriage."

"Umm," Henry groaned sleepily. "Good luck, little brother."

Maybe Henry was right. Maybe it was impossible to stay with one person. But if I thought that was true, I'd never get married at all. And I certainly wouldn't have any children I'd have to leave behind.

In the morning the pangas took us to Santiago Island to do some snorkeling. We had to lug all the gear Dad wanted Henry to test out, but most people just rented stuff on the boat. For many of them this was the first time they'd ever tried snorkeling.

What a scene on that beach! These lumpy middle-aged men and women stumbling over their flippers and wheezing into the snorkels. I kept thinking I'd hate to be Diego and be responsible for all that floating flab.

The sea lion pups, fearless as always, waddled up to check out our shoes and towels, then followed the snorkelers into the water. One old guy, coughing into his snorkel and fussing with his face mask, came face to face with a pup; it would have been hard for an unbiased observer to say which was a member of the more advanced species.

Henry was sort of a spectacle himself, wearing a tiny swimming suit, his muscles bulging out all over. I mean, I have an okay body, but I don't work at it like Henry does. Of course the Japanese girls were swarming over him — he didn't seem to mind it this morning — and I noticed even the young bride was stealing a few glances at his tanned torso.

Not everybody was snorkeling. A number of people had brought towels and books and were arranging themselves on the beach. As I started out into the water along the cliffs I saw Cat wading in the shallows. She was a stringy little creature, befitting her name, but when you saw her in a bathing suit instead of a big T-shirt, you noticed everything was in the right place.

"You're not snorkeling?" I asked.

She shook her head. "I don't swim."

I was stunned. "You mean you *can't* swim, you never learned how?"

"Yes, that's what I mean. Is that a social *faux pas* in Massachusetts?"

"No. I've just never met anybody my age who didn't know how to swim."

"Well, now you have."

"Why didn't you learn?"

"Why bother? I don't live near the ocean or any big lake or anything. You can't swim in Benson River — it's mostly white water."

"Don't they have swimming pools?"

"Of course they have swimming pools. Oregon *is* part of planet earth. Look, I had better things to do, all right? I never took lessons. I'm sure it's different where you are. All your friends are rich . . ."

"Not all my friends . . ."

"They probably spend the whole summer on Cape Cod or — "

"We go to Maine."

"Or Maine. You probably even have a sailboat back there in Kennedy country."

"Yeah, we do." But as I said it I wondered if I still had a sailboat or not. Was it Dad's boat? Who was sailing it this summer? Would we still go to Maine?

"Well, people are different, Noah. Lesson number one." She turned around and waded back to the beach to join her parents.

The fish were beautiful, but I couldn't concentrate on beauty right then. I was starting to understand that everything would be different. I wanted to figure out what this divorce was going to mean to *me*.

It meant no Maine, this summer at least. Maybe never again. Maybe Mom wouldn't want to go back there, even if she could. I knew Dad always gave Clara money and he'd paid for Henry's college education, but I also knew that Henry and Clara didn't live in the kind of house we did in Brookline. They lived in a condominium on the South Shore. I'd been there once or twice and it was nice, but I was surprised at the time how small it was. Clara worked in a bank.

Would we move out of our house now? Would Mom and I live in a little apartment? I'd be going to college in two years anyway, so maybe it didn't matter, but I loved our house. My friends were all in Brookline. Would I be able to finish high school with my friends? Suddenly everything seemed tentative. I felt like I couldn't count on anything. And I certainly couldn't count on my father or my mother, who hadn't told me the truth all these years.

I was so wrapped up in my thoughts I didn't hear Diego calling everyone to come back to shore. Henry had to come out and get me so I wouldn't miss the panga back to the boat.

After lunch we went back to explore Santiago on foot. I was amazed at how different this island looked from North Seymour. We followed a trail up from the landing beach through small bushes and dry grasses to the fur seal grottos. As we walked, Diego lectured. I followed the guy with the constantly taping videocamera, preferring to get the story in a less accurate but more amusing form.

"The reason these bushes don't have any leaves is that there are lots of wild goats on this island — two hundred thousand of them. Settlers came and brought their domesticated animals, dogs and cats and stuff like that, and then the settlers left. Or died. A lot of them died. And their animals became wild. Their children, I mean, the dog and cat descendants, are still wild, and they've destroyed lots of the original animals that lived here. Lots of species are endangered now. For instance, cats eat turtle eggs. And iguanas are like Milk-Bones or something."

Even hearing the story retold by this clown didn't make it funny. Once again, man screws up nature. Everyone moaned and shook their heads, but it occurred to me that this trail we were trampling might not be so ecologically correct either. Weren't we just another part of the problem?

We continued on to the fur seal grottos, another place it was hard to believe you were really seeing. It was like being in a National Geographic special or something. As we neared the ocean again, the land became a plain of black lava flow that stretched down the entire beach. At several places the hot lava had run out to sea and left holes that sea water rushed into. On the ledges on the sides of these holes, in little crevices, the fur sea lions lay sheltered. Diego gave some complicated explanation about all the ways they were different from other sea lions, but who's going to remember all that stuff? I could tell they were smaller than the sea lions we'd seen before and definitely furrier.

"Be a little careful," Diego warned. "There is a bull fur sea lion over there. He will protect the females and pups, so you don't want to get too close to them while he is around. One bull will patrol a whole beach full of females and pups, even though it's possible that none of them are his own offspring."

"What happens to all the other bulls?" a man asked.

"All the bulls who don't have a territory live in packs of 'bachelor' bulls. As a matter of fact, all bulls will return to the bachelor colonies for a rest after spending some weeks with these family groups." He smiled. "Can you imagine taking care of this many wives and children? You would need a rest now and then." Everybody laughed politely. But, I thought, this might be a better way to run things. A new father figure every few weeks. That way you wouldn't get so attached to one guy when he went off to find a new "territory."

The bull roared his presence and we backed farther down the beach. But he wasn't menacing us, just scaring off a smaller member of his own clan so he could have a large sunny rock to himself.

"Bully!" the elderly woman called out to him, and the group laughed nervously. Yeah, I thought, the bull gets his way. The biggest guy, the strongest guy, the oldest guy. And sometimes he might be protecting his family, but sometimes he just wants the best rock for himself. If you were a guy you might look forward to growing up and being the bull. But personally, I didn't think it looked like such an appealing role.

As the group walked on down the beach I noticed Cat lying motionless on her stomach, squinting into her camera which was pointed straight down the side of a lava cliff. I stood back and watched her for a while. She didn't move a muscle. How long could it take to get the picture?

Just then Jeremy, the eight-year-old terrorist, came thundering toward Cat, a long stick in his hand.

"Ahhhhh! Ninja warrior!" he yelled and ran right at her, then leaped over her back, still screaming.

She was on her feet before I could move. "You little monster! You ruined my shot! What the hell is wrong with you?" Cat was screaming at him.

Jeremy's mother came flying over. "What's wrong? Did something happen?"

"Can't you keep him on a rope? He could have made me drop my camera. If I'd dropped this camera into the water, that kid would be going in after it."

"For goodness sake. I'm sure it was an accident. There's no need to make a mountain out of a molehill," the mother said, leading her angel away by the hand.

I walked over, impressed. "I guess you told them."

She turned on me, still furious and shaking. "I missed the shot. It was the best picture I'd set up so far and I missed it!"

"What were you taking a picture of?"

"Only the most dramatic thing on this island! The Sally Lightfoot crabs! I had three right in front of me and the rest all fanning out behind. I was just waiting for one crab to get a little closer . . ."

Crabs? "What's a Sally Light — "

"How could you miss them! They're all over the place! Can't you see?" Steam was gushing out of her ears. "Those! Look!" She pointed down the side of the lava cliff and then turned and stomped off.

I walked closer and looked over the edge. There were easily one hundred iridescent orange crabs, each one a good eight to ten inches across, wallpapering the side of the rock. An incredible sight. And to me it still looked like a good picture. Only I didn't have a camera.

I don't think Cat took another picture on Santiago Island. She walked up front with Diego, listening intently to all his pontificating, but I could see she was still mad about missing that picture. I couldn't imagine caring so much about something like that.

"Did you see that crazy girl?" It was Jeremy, striding along next to me.

"The one you jumped over?"

"Yeah. She screamed at me. My mother says she's high-strung, but I just think she's a psycho." Jeremy, the amateur psychiatrist, was so solemn I almost laughed.

"Well," I explained, "you made her miss a picture she wanted."

"Big deal. There's pictures all over this place!" He spread his arms in a wide circle. "If that's all you want to do."

I nodded. "Gotta agree with you there, Jeremy. I guess that's why you and I don't have cameras."

Jeremy grinned up at me. "Yeah. You and me are *guys.*"

I realized I might live to regret cementing a friendship with the Santiago Screamer.

By dinnertime I was really hungry, for the first time since we got here. And I was noticing people for the first time too. There were the chipper folks who'd already made fast friends among their fellow passengers — they headed straight for the bar after dinner — and the greenish people who slurped some soup and tea, then crawled back to their cabins for another Dramamine. Then there were a number of earnest types like Cat's parents who went right down into their burrows after they ate, probably to take extensive notes on wingspread and mating habits.

I wasn't feeling so bad, and I actually considered spending some time in the bar, but looking around in there I realized I was doing the same thing everybody else was — sizing people up and deciding who to spend my fascinating personality on. Three minutes was enough to bring me back to depression. Henry beckoned

50

me to join him and the girls, each sipping a green drink through a pink straw, but I shook my head and left.

Now what? I didn't feel like hiding out in that tiny room. It seemed to me the only place to escape the happy crowd and still have room to breathe was outside, on the upper deck.

There weren't any lights on up there, just the one on the stairs which illuminated about three square feet. I guess people who like looking at the moon and the stars want it dark. Or people who want to neck.

But it was quiet when I came up the stairs so I figured I was alone. I felt my way along the railing until I was at the back of the boat. The moon reflected off the wake. It made me feel calm.

"Hi."

I just about fell over the railing.

"Jeez!" I turned around. "Who's there?"

"It's me, Cat. Did I scare you? You must not eat your carrots."

As my eyes adjusted to the darkness I could just make out the form of a person sitting in a deck chair. Great. She must have watched me feeling my way around the boat like a kid playing Pin the Tail on the Donkey.

"You didn't scare me. I just didn't see you," I said, as if that made sense.

"Sorry," she said, but I could hear her smiling.

It seemed like every time I tried to talk to this girl we ended up arguing. And I wasn't in the mood for it. I'm pretty experienced when it comes to girls. I've had girlfriends pretty steadily since the eighth grade, although the past few months I kind of let all that stuff drop.

I knew what girls liked to talk about: themselves, first

of all. After that came other girls, couples, relationships, love. I knew what they liked to do: go to movies, talk about movies, go shopping, talk about shopping. Talk some more, talk about talking. I knew what they wanted from me: to be able to say I was their boyfriend. Not to mean anything much by it, just to say it, to talk about it to everybody. There was just too much talking that didn't mean anything.

Even my mother was like that. I'd hear her telling her friends how much she *adored* me. Meanwhile she was too busy to have dinner with me more than once a week. Forget *cooking* dinner — ever. I wondered if that was another thing that would change now.

It's not that I found Cat unattractive. As a matter of fact, the more I looked at her, the better-looking she got. What was pretty about her didn't hit you right away; it kind of grew on you.

She was nothing like the girls I hung around with at home who specialized in hair-tossing and flirting. That was exciting as hell last year, but was starting to get annoying lately. I never exactly chose those girls — it just seemed like those were the ones I was *supposed* to be with. Not to brag, but I'm pretty good-looking, and people just expected me to be with girls who were that knockout kind.

Anyway, I didn't want to think about girls or relationships now. All of it was too confusing. What was the point of it? I'd just wait until I was grown up and then I'd find one really good person and get married. Maybe. Until then, why bother?

"Did you come up here to be alone?" Cat asked.

"Yeah, I guess I did."

"Me too. Should I move to the other side of the boat?"
Well, that seemed silly. "You don't have to. I mean, we can both just be quiet here, can't we?"

"Sure."

So we were quiet together. I stared down into the sparkling wake until I was practically in a trance. It was relaxing. I leaned on the railing and let the wind blow my hair back. I could almost manage to think about nothing. But I couldn't quite forget that Cat was sitting just behind me.

After maybe twenty minutes I turned around. My eyes had adjusted to the dark well enough that I could see her. She had her head back and was peering up into the stars. Almost as soon as I realized she was wrapped in a blanket, I knew I was cold.

"You ought to go get a blanket from your cabin," she said, reading my mind.

"I'm not cold," I lied, trying not to shiver. I didn't want to leave the dark. "Mind if I sit down and get out of the wind?"

"Sit," she said, waving to the chair next to hers.

I did, and leaned back to look at the stars. There must have been thousands visible way out there away from the lights of civilization. Of course, I couldn't tell one from another.

"Sorry about yelling at you this afternoon," Cat said quietly. "Nothing makes me as mad as that. When I think I've got the perfect picture and something wrecks it."

"I didn't take it personally. I figured you were still yelling at Jeremy."

"And the fates."

"I guess I don't understand photography. My dad always said a camera was a shield between a person and his life. He won't own one."

"It could be a shield, I guess. But I think of it more like editing life. I frame the good parts, the parts I want to keep, and make a perfect picture. It's a way of asking questions with your eyes. How does an iguana look with a sunset behind it? Can I freeze that hawk as he lands in the tree with his talons out? Will the mist make that hill look spooky or just hidden? Are three Sally Lightfoot crabs the perfect number in a close-up shot? I've been taking photographs for so long, my eyes work like that even without the camera. The camera taught me how to see."

Her voice had gotten jumpy and excited; she sat up straight and I could just see her hands moving through the dark, helping her explain herself. I don't know why, but it kind of knocked me out to see somebody who loved something that much.

"That sounds good," I said. "My dad could be wrong. He could definitely be wrong."

I could tell Cat was looking at me. "Are you mad at your dad?"

I don't know why I told her. I didn't intend to. I guess just because it was dark, and she'd just told me this private thing, and it seemed like she knew what I was going to say anyway.

"I hate him," I said. "He's divorcing my mother and marrying somebody else and they're having a baby."

For a long time neither of us said a word. Then she spread out her blanket and threw half of it over to me. "Here," she said. "You're freezing."

6/Cat

God, nobody's ever told me anything like *that* before. Usually when I ask questions people just tell me I'm being too nosy, or else the thing they're upset about is ridiculous anyway. The funny thing is, I'm always sort of hoping somebody will tell me a really amazing secret, like Noah did last night . . . I have this feeling people *ought* to tell me things.

But then, when Noah told me about his father leaving his family and having a baby with somebody else, I couldn't think of a thing to say! He must have just found out about it — that's why he's so moody and upset on this trip. And his father is the one who sent him on the trip — sent him away, when he didn't even want to come.

So probably I should have said something comforting, something to make him feel better. But I didn't have a clue what kind of words there were to make somebody feel better about such an awful thing. Besides, I hardly even knew this guy. Until he sat down and told me this, all we'd done was snap at each other.

I knew he was an interesting person though. I knew it that first evening at dinner. Here was this gorgeous guy staring into space and mushing up his food like a little kid. I knew there must be a story behind it.

So he dropped this news in my lap and I didn't say anything. I gave him half my blanket because he was shaking like a wet puppy. Since we were both lying back in the deck chairs, looking up, I started pointing out constellations to him. I don't even know if he was listening — I just wanted to say *something*.

"The stars are all in different places down here," I said. "There's Scorpio overhead. And the Southern Cross down over the horizon."

"I don't know much about stars," he said.

"You know the Milky Way, right? But you've never seen it like this. Usually man-made lights obscure it, but out here it lights up the whole sky."

Noah was staring up, but I wasn't sure he was seeing stars. I had a feeling he was seeing memories running on the inside screen of his eyes. After a few minutes he stood up. "I better go downstairs," he said, still shaking.

"You better take a hot shower," I said. Then I thought that was a stupid thing to say, like I'd be imagining him with his clothes off, or something.

But he just said, "Yeah, I will."

I was still trying to find the right thing to say to him. "Noah?" He turned around. "You probably won't always hate your father."

He looked at me a minute. I started to shake too, just looking at him. I'd never seen anybody look so miserable. "Maybe not. But I do now," he finally said.

If I'd shut up then, it would have been all right, but I kept blabbing. "Well, I'm glad you told me about it . . . I mean, I'm not glad it happened to you or any-thing . . . just thanks for telling me about it, I mean, you know, thank you."

Thank you? What in the hell was I thanking him for? Thank you for being so dejected that you have to talk about it to a total stranger? Thank you for injecting a little excitement into my life at your own expense? What an idiot!

I'm just not very good with boys. My girlfriends just let me be my ranting, jabbering self. They might get tired of it once in a while and say, "Cat, get off my back," or something like that, but they know that's who I am and sometimes they even appreciate me and think I'm funny. But boys all seem to want somebody different, somebody who lets *them* do all the talking, somebody who doesn't have any opinions of her own. That's not me.

I sort of have a boyfriend. Well, not really. He's my neighbor, and just a friend, which is easier, but I'd rather he was my boyfriend. I think about what it would be like to kiss him and put my arms around him. Although he chews gum all the time, which doesn't make kissing seem all that appealing. He reports back to me on his dates with Trisha and Suzanne and asks me where I think he ought to take them Saturday night and do I think a yellow corsage would look good with Annamaria's black prom dress?

Usually I'm honest, but since I totally can't stand Annamaria I said no, I thought she'd rather have something large and pink that you have to wear in your hair.

You would think I'd tell him to get lost, but no, at last report I was still getting calls from my beloved Vincent inquiring about birthday gift ideas for his latest love. I didn't yell, "What about *my* birthday, Vincent? I just turned sweet-frigging-sixteen and all I wanted was one for-God's-sake kiss so I wouldn't feel like a worthless mess of a teenage girl, but where were you, Vincent?" I knew where he was. Taking my advice and buying an amusing T-shirt for Holly — the flavor of the month — that's where.

Now this guy Noah was *way* too good-looking. He had longish blonde hair, very soft, I bet, and big brown eyes that were like magnets for anybody else's eyes. Mine anyway. I had the feeling if he smiled, he'd be deadly. Fortunately he was morbidly depressed, so I probably wouldn't have to face that terror.

Normally I pay no attention to good-looking guys. They always want to hang around with girls just like them, and, in my opinion, they have no soul. I mean, what you see is what you get. They've got no sharpness, no edges.

But last night when he was sitting next to me, shivering, Noah turned into a real person. He didn't have that bright confident look those guys have — he looked downright ruined, if you want to know the truth. And everything about him was sharp and edgy. And, damn it, when he went downstairs, I did think about him standing naked in the shower. And then I didn't even want to see him again, because I had sort of a crush on him and I figured he'd be able to spot it a mile away.

But this morning he got on the panga and nothing seemed any different. He smiled a tight little smile at me, then looked away. I found I could manage to look at him without wanting to throw myself over the side of the boat in unrequited love agonies. So I relaxed and listened to Mr. and Mrs. McNuff — parents of the adorable Jeremy McNuff who ruined my perfect shot of the Sally Lightfoot crabs yesterday — telling about their breakfast with the Baumgartners of Germany.

"The Baumgartners were telling us the most amazing

story. It seems that Mr. Baumgartner's elderly father died last year, and when he was cleaning out the papers from his desk, he came across an old journal his father had kept almost sixty years ago!" Mrs. McNuff's eyes were big and round.

"How nice for him to find something like that," my mom said.

"Wait'll you hear what was *in* it," Mr. McNuff said.

His wife took over the story again. "Seems his father had been a crewman in the 1930s for a rich man who owned a big yacht. This was when he was very young, before he was married. The yacht sailed from Germany all over the world, taking various celebrities on board —"

"Nobody I ever heard of," Mr. McNuff said.

"Well, I'm sure they were famous *then*," Mrs. McNuff said. "Anyway, the boat came here, to the Galápagos. A lot of boats came here, to Floreana Island, to visit with a mysterious Frenchwoman by the name of Jacqueline Marche."

"What was so mysterious about her?" Dad asked. He's just like me, always ready for a good mystery.

"Seems she came here with her lover. I forget his name. People were allowed to settle here in those days. The land wasn't protected as it is now," Mrs. McNuff continued. "Mr. Baumgartner's father said there were rumors that she had killed her husband before she left France, but that was never proven. Why she decided to settle in such a remote area, no one knows. And the man who came with her died in a boating accident soon after their arrival. It was all very strange. The amazing thing is, she stayed on here, by herself."

"Which is when all these rich guys from all over started

bringing their yachts here," Mr. McNuff said. "I guess she was quite good-looking."

"I'm starving!" Jeremy announced, standing up in front of his mother to reclaim her attention.

"Sit down, Jeremy. We're on a boat!" his father said.

"Honey, you'll have to wait a little while. There's no food here," his mother purred sweetly.

"But I'm hungry," he whined, his face clouding. Damn. Now we'd have to listen to him complain all morning.

"Well, you should have eaten your breakfast," his father growled.

"I didn't like that junk!" Jeremy screamed.

Now I wanted to hear about the mystery. Couldn't these people deal with their kid?

"Hey, Jeremy! Come here a minute!" I couldn't believe it. Noah was beckoning to the brat to come sit by him.

"Careful, honey," his mother said, holding onto one of his arms while Jeremy, happy to escape his father, felt his way down to Noah.

"What?"

"I thought I saw some dolphins way out there. You want to look through my binoculars and see if you can find them?"

"Really? Dad won't let me use his binoculars."

"Jeremy, please be careful with those!" his mother said.

"It's okay," Noah assured her, hanging the strap around the boy's neck.

I was pretty sure there were no dolphins this close to

shore, but Jeremy started yelling right away, "There they are! I see them!"

"What did I tell you?" Noah said, smiling, holding the kid around the waist so he didn't dump over into the water.

It was the first time I'd actually seen Noah smile, and my prediction about its fatal effect was too close for comfort. What had happened to him overnight? How come he was being such a saint with that obnoxious kid? I couldn't help looking at his hands and imagining them around *my* waist. So I looked away.

The McNuffs were finishing up their story as we got off the panga at Puerto Ayora, the main town on the most populated island, Santa Cruz.

"Sometimes somebody would get off a boat and stay on the island with Jacqueline Marche for four or five months until the boat came back for them. Mr. Baumgartner's father stayed for two years!"

"Two years!" I said. This wasn't a bad story.

"Yes! He helped her build a new house and plant crops. It's all in the journal, which Mr. Baumgartner brought along. He plans to try to find her when we get to Floreana."

"Find her? Surely she's not still alive?" Mom said.

"Yes, she is! Mr. Baumgartner wrote ahead and found some people who know her. She still lives in a little house on Floreana. Other people moved in after she did and there's a little village now. She's in her eighties, but they said she's like the unofficial mayor of the place. Sort of beloved."

"The weird thing is Baumgartner's father never said

61

a word about it to his family during his life," Mr. McNuff said. "He came home to Germany, got married, had kids, and never mentioned it. Two years he lived with this woman!" "Wouldn't you love to see that journal?" Mrs. McNuff said, rolling her eyes. "You just don't think of things like that happening in the thirties!"

Nothing intrigued me more than a good mystery. I wondered if Monique LaFarge had heard this story; it was right up her alley. I decided when we got to Floreana I'd see if I could go with the Baumgartners and find Jacqueline Marche. It was something to think about instead of just Noah and his continual transformations.

The panga arrived at the dock in Academy Bay, Puerto Ayora. After seeing nothing but deserted islands for days, it looked like a booming metropolis. The bay was full of small boats, and there were stores up and down the main street of town. There was even a bank and a small post office and a playground full of boys playing something like tether ball.

We trudged past all this and followed Diego up a long, dusty road bordered by cactus trees to the Charles Darwin Research Station. I took a lot of pictures of the trees from different angles — they were so weird — and managed to get Noah in a shot or two.

It just seemed natural to fall in beside Noah. I mean, we were the same age, and the youngest people, except for Jeremy, if you consider him a person. It seemed that Jeremy had a crush on Noah too. He stuck to him like maple syrup on pancakes.

"These are cool binoculars, Noah," the kid said. "Where'd you get 'em?"

"Oh, my dad bought them for me, for the trip," Noah said, giving me a side look I couldn't interpret.

"I'm gonna make *my* dad get *me* some."

"Maybe you could just ask him for a pair, instead of demanding them," I suggested. Jeremy looked at me like I was a virus.

"Me and Noah are talking," he pointed out.

The McNuffs finally started to feel a little guilty, I guess, about giving custody of their kid to Noah, and they came around to claim him. "Give Noah his binoculars back," his mother said.

"How come I don't have any binoculars?" Jeremy said. "You never get stuff for me!"

"Get me! Get me! Is that all you can say?" his dad yelled, yanking his arm.

"There's a snack bar just up the road, Jer-Jer. Would you like a candy bar? Or a Coke?" His mother pried his arm away from his father and held it gently.

"I guess so," the formerly starving Jeremy said, and allowed himself to be led off.

"Poor kid," Noah said, shaking his head. "I hope he gets to stay with his mother after the divorce."

"His parents are getting a divorce?"

Noah shrugged. "That's what it says in *my* crystal ball."

I had been thinking that the parents were the ones to be pitied here, but I guessed I could see Noah's point. "Are your parents like that?" I asked.

Noah looked surprised, like he'd forgotten what he'd told me last night. But then he said, "No, not at all. In fact, I always thought they were perfect parents. With the perfect marriage. I guess I wasn't paying much attention, was I?"

"Well, maybe it was a perfect marriage once."

Noah turned on me. "Explain that to me. How can somebody have a perfect marriage, and then suddenly it's not? Suddenly it's so rotten you have to run away from it and find somebody else to love! Explain that to me! Because I don't get it!"

I must have been standing there with my mouth open. How could I explain anything to anybody? What I knew about love was filed under Complete Fantasy.

Noah shook his head. "I'm sorry. It doesn't have anything to do with you. This whole thing just has me so . . . screwed up." He took his baseball cap off and ran his hand angrily through his hair.

It's awful when that feeling of, I don't know — caring, wanting, needing, whatever it is — it's awful when it washes over you all of a sudden, and makes you feel hot and silly and not good enough. I'd had it once or twice with Vincent, but never this bad, never so bad that I thought I'd burst into tears right there because I wasn't the right girl to reach over and take his hand.

And then just as I was feeling like a bowl of leftovers, Noah turned that famous smile on me. "How come you always get to ask all the questions? How about you? Your parents seem to be happy together. Are they?"

"I guess I never thought about it." It was hard to think about my parents at a time like this. "Sure, they get along."

"That's all? They just get along?"

"Well, there's probably more to it than I see. I mean, they don't go around kissing each other all the time or anything like that. But they don't argue too much either." I thought about how, most nights, they stood in the kitchen, discussing sauces and stove temperatures, cooking dinner together. Sometimes on the weekend they'd spend a whole day baking bread. "Yeah, I think they probably do have a good marriage."

"Do you think people are destined for one another?"

I had to look off at the cactus trees and away from his eyes in order to come up with an answer. "I don't know about destiny, but I do believe in" — clear your throat, how are you going to be able to say this word? — "I mean, love." I said it and I didn't die, although possibly my face was as bright as the cherry on top of a sundae.

Noah scowled. "Love, huh? Have you ever been in love? I haven't. I mean I've dated a lot of girls and I thought I was in love once or twice, but now I don't think I was."

I pulled myself together and tried to figure out how to rearrange Vincent into a love object. How could I tell Noah I'd never been in love, never even dated anybody? He'd think I was a completely naive little dork.

"Well, there is a guy I like a lot." That much was true.

"Yeah, yeah, we all *like* people. I said *love*. Do you love him?"

I *had* to lie. It seemed like the only way to keep the truth to myself. "Yes, I think so."

"And you can imagine never loving anybody else your whole life except this one guy — what's his name?"

"Vincent."

"Never loving anybody but Vincent forever. That would be enough?"

Just me and Vincent living in a trailer court off Highway 5, tooling around in his rusty '76 Dodge with the muffler falling off while he ogled Barbie look-alikes out the window. Suddenly I couldn't imagine why I'd found Vincent even remotely attractive.

"I think so," I smiled, deception curling my upper lip.

Noah was quiet a minute, staring at the dusty road. "Maybe women are a higher life form than men."

"No maybe about it. It's scientific fact!" I was glad to drop the subject of Vincent. I hated lying to people, especially Noah.

"Yeah. That's what my mom and her friends think, too. As soon as Dad was out of the house women came swarming in from all over, like ants to a picnic. It was halfway between a wake and a party for about two weeks. One minute somebody'd be in tears and the next minute they'd all be shrieking with laughter."

Noah's voice got very low. Anger sprang up again from its hidden source. "But whether they were laughing or crying you could be sure why: *men*. All of whom are apparently just the same: thoughtless, stupid, and incapable of love."

Wow. "I was just kidding," I said quietly, but Noah wasn't listening.

"I could walk past and they'd look up and say, 'Hi, Noah! How's school? You playing tennis this year?' Like we were old pals. Then, while I'd still be within earshot they'd say, 'Men are more trouble than they're worth. Who needs them?'

"The big joke was, if they can send one man to the moon, why can't they send all of them? They howled over that one. And I'm right there! I'm the scum they can't wait to get rid of!"

We'd stopped walking. Noah was scuffing at the dirt with his sneaker like a bull looking for a fight.

I knew what Noah meant. I'd heard girls talk about boys that way too. But was that any more insulting than boys making comments about a girl's looks or the size of her breasts?

"Don't you think they were just trying to make your mom feel better? Like it wasn't her fault. Even *you* blame your dad — that's what you said!"

"Yes, I *do* blame him. But that doesn't mean all men are plague-carrying rats."

"I'm sure they didn't mean you."

"Well, it sure felt like they meant me."

Short of begging him to be my own personal disease-infested rodent, I couldn't think of anything consoling to say. After a few minutes of listening to his angry silence I said, "You play tennis?"

He was startled by the new subject. "Yeah. Do you?"

"No courts in Benson River. You have to belong to the country club in Redburg."

He nodded.

"So, do you wear all white when you play?"

"Usually. Why?"

I shrugged. "I don't know. 'You playing tennis this year?' It sounded so *eastern* or something. I could just picture you."

A smile flicked at his lips. "And when you pictured me was I winning or losing?"

"Well, you were behind until Martina Navratilova accused you of spreading bubonic plague . . ."

Noah laughed and caught my hand in his for just a minute which practically caused total paralysis of the left side of my body.

"Sorry," he said.

"No reason to be."

"Let's go. We're missing your pal, Diego, and his immortal turtle speech."

"*Tortoises*, not turtles," I corrected him.

"Whatever."

The group was assembled in front of pens of baby giant tortoises. I moved away from Noah, because standing near him was so distracting, and I really wanted to hear what Diego had to say. Besides, we were supposed to find out today what made Diego a big hero around here. I didn't intend to miss it.

It was hard to believe these little six-inch-long creatures would someday weigh five hundred pounds. I put the telephoto lens on the camera so I could get some close-ups of their heads. The eyes were amazing, the heavy lids closing over them like a slow curtain. Even the baby ones seemed to have eyes that had seen things for a hundred years.

As soon as Diego started to talk about the tortoises, he came alive. You could see this was where he ought to be; he loved the place.

"At one time there were *hundreds of thousands* of Galápagos tortoises on these islands. Now there are less than fifteen thousand. Many tortoise eggs are eaten by the packs of feral animals that now roam the islands. But the greater harm was done when they were taken in large numbers by the whaling ships that sailed the Pacific Ocean in the first half of the nineteenth century. One ship might take anywhere from one hundred to six hundred tortoises at a time, keeping them alive until they were needed for food — an endless supply of fresh meat."

Mr. McNuff chuckled. "Mighty tough meat, I bet. It probably took so long to chew it, they forgot they were hungry!"

A few other people laughed too, but most of us saw the look on Diego's face. When he spoke again he sounded so mad, you'd have thought those whalers left just last week. "It is estimated that more than two hundred thousand tortoises were taken from the islands during those years, Mr. McNuff. Environmental destruction is not really so amusing." He stared at the guy a minute and then continued. "Each of the islands of the Galápagos had its own distinct subspecies of tortoise. Many of these subspecies are endangered, which is why we bring the existing tortoises here to the Research Station to breed in safety. For years we thought that four of the original fifteen subspecies were completely extinct."

A nervous smile played around Diego's mouth as he called to a man working inside the incubator area. "Over there is my friend Andre. Four years ago Andre and I found eggs belonging to one of the species thought to be extinct."

7/ Noah

This Diego guy sure knows how to play to an audience. First he gives this furious speech about how humans have killed off whole species of these rare giant turtles, or rather tortoises, and then he announces that he and some other guy singlehandly saved one whole species. I guess that's why he's a saint around here. Then he gives this modest little smile while the whole flock of Albatrosses practically lifts him to their shoulders. Even Cat was tripping over her lower jaw.

I admit it's a good story. Apparently four years ago Diego and his pal Andre had just come to work for the Research Station. They were sent to some of the small islands to look for tortoise bones for some kind of comparative research. Nobody thought there were any live tortoises left. But sure enough, they got to this one little island, Casanova Island, and found a cache of eggs lying near the carcass of the turtle that must have been the mother. There were feral cats digging up the eggs and eating them — that's what alerted these guys to the nest. They chased the cats away and managed to bring four unbroken eggs back to the Research Station for incubation. They searched the island thoroughly, but never found another turtle, not even one who might have fathered the eggs.

So the tortoises are kind of famous now. Diego took us to see them; they have their own pen with a big sign over it that says THE ORPHAN TORTOISES OF CASANOVA. The whole story is written up on posters with pictures of Diego and Andre. The tortoises are now about two-thirds the size they will be when fully grown. Apparently there's a big celebration planned for next week when Diego and Andre return the tortoises to Casanova Island to try to repopulate it. The *Santiago* passengers get to go to it, too.

Diego didn't seem all that excited about it, though — he was almost nervous telling us about the celebration plans. Maybe he doesn't want to take them back. Maybe he won't be such a hero once the "orphan tortoises" have left the Research Station.

For some reason I just don't trust the guy — he seems sneaky to me. But he's some kind of minor god to everybody else. If he's such a great tortoise researcher, what's he doing leading tourists around all day? Even Cat had to admit she'd wondered about that.

Cat's a strange girl. I was a little worried about seeing her today after blurting out my story last night. She was very nice about it at the time, not shocked or anything, but she probably wondered why I told her. I don't really know myself. But I'm not sorry I did.

I just needed to tell somebody, to say it out loud. And for some reason I trust Cat. She's not like my friends at home. They're always serious about the small stuff, like cars and tests and who's dating who, but they wouldn't know how to deal with a real crisis, especially somebody else's. Cat seems just the opposite. She's in her own goofy world half the time, taking pictures of everything in sight, but when you want to talk seriously, she's very thoughtful. I mean, full of thoughts. She listens and then she tells you right out what she thinks. Even when she doesn't agree with me, she doesn't make me feel like a rotten person.

She's in love with some guy named Vincent. I don't really have anything in common with her anyway. As a matter of fact she was driving me nuts this afternoon making up a bunch of crazy stories.

"Look at Mr. Honeymoon," she said. She's got these names for everybody. "He must have eight hours of video by now of Mrs. Honeymoon just standing in front of motionless animals saying, 'I'dn that cute?' They're going to have to *pay* people to sit and watch this."

"The snoring will be symphonic," I said.

"You know who Mr. Honeymoon is *really* interested in?" Cat whispered. "Monique LaFarge."

"Who?"

"She's a Dolphin. You've seen her on the boat. The tall blonde French woman with the beautiful accent."

"Her? She's too old for him. What makes you think — "

"Calm down, Noah. I'm imagining. Don't you think they'd make a good couple? She's rich so she can get an apartment in New York where his business takes him quite often . . ."

I started to get mad. "This is a little too close to home to be amusing, Cat. I don't see the humor."

She looked startled. "I'm sorry. I didn't think of that. I just let anything happen when I'm pretending. They're just stories. I like to imagine all the possibilities in life. I mean, anything can happen."

"Great. But married men having affairs isn't a story I want to imagine right now."

"You're right. I guess because nothing real ever happens to me, I like the stories." She looked downright sad.

"What do you mean, nothing real ever happens to you? You're on a boat in the Galápagos Islands, right?"

She smiled, almost shyly, and her eyes sparkled.

"And you're in love with Vincent, right? Isn't that enough?"

The smile faded out a little. "Vincent. Sure."

"Look, do somebody else. How about them?" I pointed to an elderly couple who'd just passed us, the woman holding onto the man's arm. I would have bet on my parents looking like that in thirty years. Before I wised up.

She brightened. "Oh, the Moneypennys! I already have a story for them. He's dying of a rare incurable disease and she stands to inherit a lot of money, but he's not dying fast enough and she's tired of waiting. Besides, he's a pain in the neck. So she's trying to figure out a way of bumping him off while they're on this trip. I wouldn't be surprised if he has a little accident concerning the railing of the ship. Or maybe she gets the Dramamine mixed up with the rat poison."

I had to laugh. "And she looks so kind. Like an old sea lion."

"Never trust that kind."

"No, I won't. I may never trust anybody for that matter." It was supposed to be a joke, but Cat didn't laugh.

"This is supposed to be a game. You keep making it real."

"Sorry." I shrugged.

"I feel stupid doing this with you. When you have a real life that's so dramatic."

"Let's not do it then," I said. If she could be blunt, so could I.

"Fine," she said, and took off towards her favorite guide. Since there was nothing else to do, I followed.

The Albatrosses were gathered under a small roof looking over a railing at one lone turtle hiding in the underbrush. Diego was blabbing again.

"The tortoise you see here is the last living representative of the sub-species *abingdoni* from Pinta Island. Researchers have not been able to find another tortoise like him. We call him Lonesome George; when he dies, another sub-species of tortoise will be extinct."

For some reason this got to me. He was the last one. I stood and looked at him a long time.

People asked questions. Nobody knew how old he was, Diego said. Or how long he'd live. Yes, they'd tried to interest him in other female tortoises, but he refused them. I don't know, I felt so sorry for the guy. He was waiting for the right girl, but he was never going to find her.

I stood and watched him while the rest of the group went on to another pen. It seemed like I couldn't look away from him. Very slowly his head came out of his big, dusty shell and it kept coming until that long, wrinkled neck seemed more like a big snake that had been coiled inside the shell. He picked a leaf off a bush and slowly pulled himself back inside. He started to move his thick, tree-trunk feet, turning in a circle away from me, like he couldn't stand to have me watch him anymore.

I wanted to apologize to him. Not that it was my fault his group didn't evolve fast enough to escape the whalers, didn't sprout long legs to run away, or poisonous bites or protective coloration or something. It just made me kind of sick to stand there and see this one lonely creature, the last of his kind, and to think that human beings did this, without a second thought. What was the matter with people that they didn't think who or what was going to be hurt before they blundered stupidly on, doing whatever they felt like doing?

Cat came trudging back towards me. "We're walking back into town now. We get to eat on the island today. I'm so hot I could — "

The anger was creeping up my throat and I had to spit it out, even though Cat was the only person there.

"These poor buggers are lucky they aren't *all* extinct by now! Why do they trust us? Why do they let us run around here staring at them and making videotapes? We're not to be trusted! How long does it take to develop enough fear to save your life?"

I was afraid the sympathy I saw in her eyes might be for me, so I turned around and ran down the road, alone, all the way into town.

8/Cat

Since we're docked off Santa Cruz for a few days a band from Puerto Ayora came on board after dinner and set up in the bar. They moved some of the tables aside so there was room for dancing, even though the music wasn't like anything I'd ever heard before, all sorts of flutes and drums.

There were five men in the band, all dressed in brightly colored, striped ponchos and white pants. They played instruments I'd never even seen before, tiny little guitar-type things and bamboo pipes tied together from smallest to largest. The way they played them reminded me of the way you play a soda bottle with your top lip held out over it.

I didn't intend to dance, but the music was pretty. Even Mom and Dad stayed around to listen for a while. I didn't sit with them though, not that they noticed. It's odd; I've been trying to avoid hanging around with them on this trip, thinking they'd want us to go everywhere as a family, like always. But they didn't seem to care if I joined them or not!

They were sitting at this little table for two — like what if I *wanted* to sit with them? — and Dad actually had his *arm* around Mom! I guess it's kind of romantic to be on a boat sailing around a bunch of islands. Just ask the Romeo and Juliet of Benson River, Oregon.

Anyway, it was fine with me. I put on my long skirt, since it seemed like a special evening with the band and all. At the last minute I grabbed my camera. Just in case everybody else got up to dance I could walk around taking pictures and not look like a dork just waiting to be asked. I remembered what Noah's father said about people hiding behind their cameras. A useful idea!

I stood in the back for a few minutes, listening, and taking pictures of the band. I certainly didn't want to sit with my parents, and I wasn't sure I'd have the nerve to march up to Noah's table either, even if I could find him. He'd hardly spoken to me all afternoon, and I was tired of trying to figure out what I thought of him, the Jekyll and Hyde of Brookline, wherever that was.

Then I noticed Henry the Third was whirling Miyoko

around the dance floor. Tomoko and Sachiko were sitting at a table by themselves, looking a bit glum. Who better to sit with? All we needed was a neon sign flashing over the table: ORPHAN WALLFLOWERS OF THE M/V SANTIAGO.

"Mind if I sit here?" I asked.

They both smiled. "Yes, please," Sachiko said. "You liking dance?"

I pulled up a chair. "No, I'm not much of a dancer. I just like to listen to the music. Do you dance?"

Tomoko made a face. "We liking dance very much, but no mens like us to dance."

That creepy Henry, I thought. Even if he's decided he likes Miyoko best, he could at least dance with the other girls a few times.

"Do you like Henry?" I asked, coming right to the point.

"We like Henry?" Tomoko said. She looked at Sachiko and they both laughed heartily. No more girlish giggles. "We like Henry?" she repeated.

"You don't?"

"Henry like big baby wants have all toys in own crib," Tomoko said. "He think all girls crazy with him. Henry wise as turkey!" She crossed her eyes and Sachiko howled with laughter.

"So I guess you're not too fond of him?"

"He big silly American. But Miyoko like very much. She say we don't give chance to big Henry. What you think? You like brother of Henry?"

God, did everybody on the boat have me figured out? "Well, yes, I like his brother more than I like Henry. But then, I've never really spoken to Henry much. I guess he likes to . . . have a good time."

Tomoko and Sachiko both thought that was scream-ingly funny, too.

"Wish more boys on boat for us. Too many old people. How old Henry brother?"

"Um, Noah is sixteen. Like I am."

They looked at each other. "Sixteen. We eighteen, but he . . . how say . . . pretty?"

"Handsome," I corrected her. "Good-looking."

"Yes! Looking good!" I had to laugh with them this time. Here I'd been feeling sorry for them, assuming they *wanted* to be hanging around with Henry, when they had the guy's number all along. I was a little discon-certed, however, that they were now interested in Noah.

"Hey! Look who's at our table! It's Kitty-Cat!" Who else could it be but Henry, depositing Miyoko in a chair and grinning at me. "Let me get you something to drink! Anybody else?"

Why not? We all let Henry get us a soft drink. I was thirsty, and anyway, Henry seemed to enjoy pretending he was a cavalier slave to women.

"You girlfriend Henry brother?" Miyoko asked me.

"No! I just met him."

She nodded. "I girlfriend Henry now. Sachiko say Henry have many girlfriend." She shrugged. "Maybe so. Maybe I make best girlfriend."

Tomoko batted her hand at Miyoko. "How you be best? You going Japan one more week."

"You see. Henry rich. He come see me."

Tomoko and Sachiko stopped rolling their eyes only when Henry returned with our drinks.

"Thank you, Henry, who save all Japanese girls from loneliness!" Sachiko said sweetly, with no trace of sarcasm. I had to take a big drink of ginger ale to keep from breaking up.

"You bring camera," Miyoko said, pointing to it. "You please would take picture of Henry and Miyoko?"

"Sure," I said.

Henry grimaced. "Don't we have enough pictures already?"

"You take good pictures. I give you my address Japan and you send to me. I send you something back from Japan," Miyoko continued.

"Sounds good," I said, getting them in focus.

Henry gave up and put his arm around Miyoko, flashing his usual big smile. But Miyoko didn't smile. She leaned her head back against Henry's chest and looked wistful. It was as perfect a picture as the one I'd lost of the Sally Lightfoot crabs. I had no doubt I was taking a picture of love.

"Listen! A waltz! Kitty-Cat, how about dancing with me?" Henry said, breaking away from Miyoko.

"No! Really, I don't dance very well, especially to something like this."

"Oh, it's easy. I can teach you in no time."

If there's anything I hate it's being taught how to do something in public. "Really, I can't . . ."

"Never say can't, Kitty-Cat!"

"Look, I won't budge from this chair unless you stop calling me Kitty-Cat. Cat is fine, although I may force you to go back to Catherine just so you don't slip up."

Henry smiled and took my hand. He was so good at this stuff. "Cats are light on their feet, you know." As he led me onto the dance floor, I caught a glimpse of the sour look on Miyoko's face.

"You trying to make your girlfriend jealous?" I asked as he pulled me close.

"Is she my girlfriend? Relax and follow me. It's one, two, three, one, two, three . . . that's right."

"She seems to think she is," I said, following the easy steps. "I guess she's just the pick of the litter while you're on the boat, huh? Nothing serious."

Henry gave me an odd look. "I don't get serious. But I like Miyoko."

"Do you?"

He shrugged. "Sure. Besides, she likes me."

I laughed. "Don't your girlfriends *usually* like you?"

Henry smiled his most charming smile, which had undoubtedly been turned on many a female before me. I could see why it got results, though I preferred Noah's lower-wattage looks.

"Well, they *act* like they do, of course. In the dance of dating, they know all the steps."

"And so do you."

"And so do I."

"And Miyoko doesn't."

Another big smile. "She's a serious girl. I like her, but I don't want her to get her hopes up, if you know what I mean."

"Boys just want to have fun, right?"

"You got it, Pussycat," he said, pulling me in closer. I might have to change my name.

The waltz was the one dance Mom and Dad could do, and they'd taught me when I was little. But it was different doing it with Henry. I felt self-conscious when our bodies bumped together, and I didn't know what to do with my face. When he pulled me close to him, I'd either have to smother in his shirt or crane my neck backwards to look up at him. Neither was an appealing choice. I pulled back a little.

"I swear," Henry said, "I don't know what's wrong with my little brother. I had you picked out for him from day one, but where is he? He should be waltzing you across the equator, not me."

"Don't feel you have to atone for your brother's mistakes," I said, a little nastily, but Henry thought that was a riot too.

"You're really cute, you know that?"

Oh, God, why didn't I just stay in my room tonight? Henry pulled me in for a fast swirl and I stumbled over his feet. Suddenly he stopped dancing; I assumed I'd injured him, and felt no remorse whatsoever.

"Hey Noah!" Henry pulled me across the floor until we were standing toe to toe with his brother. "Here's somebody you ought to be dancing with, Bro. Because she's too smart for me!"

"Sure." Noah smiled a tight-lipped smile and led me away from Henry.

"We don't have to dance. Your brother is . . . " Better not to say.

"My brother is what?" Noah looked interested.

What the heck? "Your brother is a jerk sometimes."

Noah smiled. "I know. But he's a nice jerk."

We started to dance, not so close up and wild like with Henry. Just slow and steady; even though I was nervous, I could enjoy it.

"You're a good dancer," I said.

"It's part of the curriculum for being rich in Brookline," he said. "I'm polite to my elders too."

"I'm sure you are. Now if you could only master being polite to people your own age."

He just smiled and gazed off over my shoulder. I wished I knew what was normal behavior for this guy — being sweet or screaming at people for no good reason.

"Miyoko likes your brother," I said.

"Too bad for her. Henry plays the field. He's like my dad. He'll never have just one woman."

"Too bad for him."

"Yeah, too bad for him." Really talkative tonight.

"Noah, about what you said this morning, about how the animals shouldn't trust people . . ."

I could feel his body tighten; his hand gripped mine so hard it hurt. "Forget it. It was just seeing that last turtle, all alone. I felt responsible."

"Well, that's what I was going to say. In a way, we *are* responsible. And we're taking that responsibility. People are, I mean. The whole Darwin Research Station was set up to protect the tortoises."

"We wouldn't have to protect them if we hadn't destroyed half of them already."

"Maybe so, but that doesn't make all humans evil. Think of it this way. If you could boil all human beings down into one person with good impulses and bad impulses — which all of us have, right? — as long as the good side finally takes control of things, you're okay."

He gave me a lopsided grin. "And you think the good side is now in control, do you?"

"I hope so. I can't read the future."

"In the future all human beings will be boiled down into one person." He gave me an actual full-blown smile which was as hard to look right into as the equatorial sun.

The music stopped and Captain Bolmeier, wearing a snazzy white uniform tonight, with long pants, stepped up to the microphone. "Ladies and gentlemen, Meine Damen und Herren, damas y caballeros, while the band takes a short break, I invite you all to have a complimentary cocktail with your captain's pleasure." It sure would make you think twice before you made a big announcement if you had to repeat it three times. Still, when you watched him swaggering around the boat in those silly knee socks, you got the feeling that waking people up and announcing free drinks was about all he was good for.

But tonight he had more to say. "I know everyone visited the Darwin Research Station today, and now you know our secret! The *M/V Santiago* is privileged to have a researcher of the status of Diego Alvarado on board. Let's give him a round of applause!"

Of course we had to applaud in three separate groups too, which took a while, but still Diego didn't show up to take his bows. The captain was looking around for him. Noah sighed disgustedly. For some reason, he didn't seem to like Diego.

The captain still wasn't finished — he was going for the Pulitzer Prize in translation here. "Next Friday morning you are all invited to join in the festivities when the orphan tortoises of Casanova are returned to their home island. After the ceremonies there will be a fiesta on the ship!"

This was greeted with lots of hooraying, while everybody scrambled to the bar for their free drink.

"You want to go outside a minute? Get some air?" Noah asked. I wished I didn't have the feeling that I would follow him over the side of the boat if that was his suggestion.

"Sure, I said, shrugging, like it was no big deal.

But almost as soon as we stepped outside we could hear voices from up on the top deck. It was so dark we couldn't see who it was, but the woman was obviously angry.

"Why do you have to stay on the boat tomorrow night?" she said.

"I told you. I'm in charge of crew schedules for next week and I need to get them finished," the man said.

"Well, can't you finish it up tonight? Then you can come with me. It's a party at Lourdes' house. How often do we happen to be docked at Santa Cruz when someone I know is giving a party in Puerto Ayora?"

"Sofia, I'm sorry. Not this time. I can't."

Sofia. I looked at Noah.

"Your pal, Diego," he whispered. "And his girl-friend."

I know we should have gone back inside; Noah would have, but I grabbed his arm. "Wait!" I said.

"We're eavesdropping!"

"You and your manners," I whispered. "Think of it as research on your own species," I said. He sighed, but didn't leave.

Sofia was taking no prisoners. "Diego, what is the matter with you? You have hardly spoken to me all week! Do you want to break up with me? Is that it?"

"Of course not, Sofia! Don't be ridiculous!"

"Because I won't beg you to stay with me! If I go to that party by myself there will be men surrounding me like mosquitos! I don't need you to —"

"Sofia, please! Don't torture me. You know I love you." Diego sounded as tortured as Harrison Harding was a couple of months ago when Dina Knight was leaving him on my favorite soap, *Always Another Morning*, which I'd never admit to anyone I watch. Only hearing somebody say it like this, in the dark, for real, standing next to Noah, it was all I could do not to close my eyes and drift to the floor.

"I don't know anything of the kind," Sofia said. "You men, you think you just have to say, 'I love you,' and women will fall to their knees."

Obviously true of me, I thought, my jellied joints threatening to give way any minute.

Noah snickered. "That's right, Sofia, don't buy it!"

"He *does* love her. Can't you tell?" I said.

"I'm just asking you to trust me this one time, Sofia. I have something I must do tomorrow night. You go to the party and have a good time. But remember that the man who loves you is on this ship."

"Right," Noah said. "And if you believe that, I've got some nice desert land you might be interested in." He turned to leave. "I've had enough. Are you coming back in?"

I shook my head. "Can't. Have to hear the ending."

Noah disappeared through the door, shaking his head. Oh well. I didn't intend to miss the kiss.

Sofia snickered. "Who loves me? Captain Bolmeier? Or do you mean that muscly American boy with enough snorkeling equipment for an army?"

"You know who I mean." Diego breathed the words heavily and I imagined him burying his face in her hair.

The sound of the slap was louder than I would have thought flesh on flesh could be.

"Do you think I'm an idiot, Diego? I can tell when a man is lying to me! You stay here and I will go to the party. But don't think you will ever be kissing me again!"

"Sofia!" he shouted.

I crawled quickly into the shadows behind a post. Sofia stomped angrily down the stairs and disappeared inside. This was not going to be the night I learned about love.

9/Noah

What a nerve that girl has! Sitting right there listening to people arguing. I admit it was kind of fascinating for a few minutes, but hasn't she ever heard of privacy? I can just imagine Julie Latham or one of the other girls from my class in that situation — she'd say, "Oh, gross!" like anything romantic was a big hoot. She'd make a face like she'd just smelled something rotten.

Cat brought all her camera gear along this morning for the trip to the highlands on Santa Cruz. This photography stuff was the most important thing in the world to her.

When we got off the pangas at the dock we had to get on these rickety old blue buses that belched black smoke for the entire hour ride up to the highlands. Once we got out of Puerto Ayora the road was empty except for a pickup truck or two, a man on horseback and a bunch of kids running along the side. Some of the land was being farmed; it was lush and ferny.

I kept thinking you could grow up here and be so safe. You could fall backwards into the soft weeds like a kid making snow angels. You could be happy not even knowing about snow.

The buses finally stopped at a clearing where the trail to the pit craters began. Up here it was actually raining and I wished I had worn more than a T-shirt. But the rain was so fine you didn't really get wet, just moist . . . it was kind of nice after the daily heat of the flatter islands.

The trail had the feeling of a rain forest; the ground was thick with all sorts of exotic plants and ferns and there were mossy vines hanging from the trees. Cat was looking for a bird called the vermilion flycatcher, so she stayed near the front of the single-file column with Diego. She said she thought he'd probably spot one first, but I knew she'd happily use any excuse to march up front with her fearless leader. Especially now that she knew he'd been dumped by his girlfriend.

I stayed near the back of the group, but by the oohs and aahs I figured they'd probably tracked their prey. By the time the last of us maneuvered up the trail, there was no little red bird to be seen. But when I caught up to Cat at the pit craters, she was mad.

"Damn! I had the wrong lens on the camera! Can you believe it? I am so stupid, I don't deserve to have this camera." She was steaming.

"Maybe you'll see another one on the walk back," I said.

"Not like this. I took the best shots and now I realize I had a wide-angle lens on here!"

"Hey, it's a bird. Don't stroke out. Besides, while you've got the wide-angle lens on, you ought to be taking pictures of this!" Before us lay an enormous volcanic crater, its sides covered with fuzzy trees that looked like giant stalks of broccoli, the mist swirling just above.

Cat was quiet a minute, looking over the scene. "You're right," she said quietly. "Thanks."

I watched her pace back and forth around the edge of the crater, her eye glued to the viewfinder, and I wondered how she knew when she had the perfect shot. Why click the shutter at one spot and not the other? But I could tell it wasn't random. She trusted herself to know which picture would be right. It must be nice to be that good at something.

Meanwhile, Diego was lecturing us on the formation of the pits. I figured as long as I was there I might as well listen to him instead of wasting my time with that videocamera guy. This stuff does get more interesting when you understand it.

"At one time this was all lava up to the top. But because of volcanic action under the surface, an empty space was created and the surface lava fell in on itself forming these craters which are several acres wide." Boy, the guy really seemed weird today. He kept fidgeting with his hands, sticking them in his pockets, then wiping them on his pants, folding them together behind his back — he couldn't hold still.

On the trek back through the forest Cat did have another chance for vermilion flycatcher pictures, though she claimed the one she missed would have been the best. I saw the bird this time too, its bright red chest brilliant against the grayish-green trees. It sat on a branch right in front of us for several minutes, tipping its head right and left, posing, I thought.

It was funny how much I was enjoying this trip. I never thought I cared particularly about birds or sea lions or exotic trees, or even endangered animals. But it was very easy to be here. The scenery wasn't flashy, it was just what it was — practically unspoiled islands full of things I'd never seen or thought about before.

Everything in my life was changing. I didn't even know how much of a change yet, but I knew it would be major. But here was a quiet place to be myself and think about how everything in the world fit together. Maybe Dad wasn't so dumb sending me off to the middle of nowhere. I felt like I belonged here.

We had lunch at a ranch about halfway down the hill going back into town. Diego pulled Sofia aside and tried to get her to go for a walk with him. I could see him motioning towards a trail, but she must have given him a very short answer. Next thing I knew she'd joined a group of people playing volleyball.

The afternoon was free. We could do as we pleased, wander through town, visit the lava tubes, or go back to the Darwin Station. There was a handful of shops in Puerto Ayora and it looked like most of the Albatrosses and a good many of the other birds and beasts as well were headed for those.

"You going shopping?" I asked Cat, figuring maybe we could pick up a souvenir or two.

"No, I want to take pictures," she said, her eyes constantly scanning as though some shot might get away from her if she wasn't on the lookout.

"You took pictures all morning," I griped.

"I'm feeling good now. With the camera, I mean. I'm kind of on a roll or something."

I gave up. "Okay. See you later."

Most of the stores were big on T-shirts. Since my mom has everything she needs anyway, I got her a shirt with mother and baby sea lions on it. I knew she'd at least like the idea of it, even if she never wore it. I bought myself a shirt with an albatross on it — it seemed appropriate. I wasn't going to buy anything for my dad — why did he need a present; he was getting everything he wanted anyway — but then I went back and bought him a shirt too, a blue-footed booby shirt. I was very proud of myself.

In another store I bought a handful of postcards, though there was no one I felt like sending them to. I thought I should send one to my mother, but I'd probably be home before she got it anyway. I chose pictures I thought I'd like to have myself, to remember the place. Since I didn't have a camera.

This vast amount of shopping took me about half an hour. I still had the whole afternoon to kill. I'd seen Henry walk by with Miyoko, which probably meant Sachiko and Tomoko were looking for something to do — maybe I could find them. But then what? Sit around some bar drinking Coke all afternoon? Besides, in some funny way Sachiko and Tomoko reminded me of the girls I dated back home. It wouldn't matter to them who I was — they just wanted to hang out with a guy.

I kind of hated to admit it, but weird as she was, I'd rather spend the afternoon with Cat.

So I went looking. Where would she go, I wondered. She wouldn't stay on the main road that goes through town — too many tourists, not enough atmosphere. She might have gone back down to the docks — there was some life happening there, but I suspected she would take off on a new road, someplace she hadn't been before. Sure enough. I turned off the main road onto a dirt road that ran up between some small houses. There she was, crouching behind a bush, taking pictures of chickens in somebody's back yard.

I couldn't imagine that these were prize-winning chicken pictures, but I knew by now not to interrupt her when she was shooting something. I waited until she took the camera away from her face.

"I found you," I said.

She jumped. "Oh! I didn't know you were there!"

"I figured out where you'd go and I was right."

"Oh, really? Where would I go?" She put one hand on her jutted-out hip and brushed her thick hair out of her face with the other one. Standing there glaring at me, she looked really terrific.

"Down some road like this, where there aren't any tourists. Where you can commune with the chickens."

"Noah, if you're making fun of me, I don't appreciate it."

"What?"

"You're always making some crack about how backwoods I am."

"That's not what I meant at all . . ."

"You think I'm a hick because I don't know about German poets — "

"I never said you were a hick! Jeez. What's the matter with you? You put the wrong lens on your camera again?"

She glared for another few seconds, but then her frown turned into a smile. "My battery's running low. I missed this great shot . . ." She pointed toward the chickens.

"Your battery's running low? Your battery's running low? That's why you lit into me like a mad dog?"

She laughed and put her head down, her hair swinging like a sheet of silk. "I'm sorry, but when something like this happens . . ."

I advanced on her, grabbed her by the arms and gave her a playful shake. "Your battery's running low? Is that what you said?"

This was the kind of stuff, horseplay my mother called it, that I did with my friends at home. It gave guys an excuse to touch girls, but it was just kidding around. The girls giggled and screamed and tried to run away and you chased them. I haven't done much of it since I started actually taking girls on dates, where you get to touch them without all the excuses.

I should have known Cat wouldn't be the giggling, running-away type. Instead she just looked right into my eyes with that big smile still on her lips. I totally forgot that I'd sworn off girls. And I was just about to lean down and kiss her, *kiss* this crazy girl, when I suddenly remembered Vincent, her one and only true love.

So I let her go and backed away, both of us kind of embarrassed. What would she have done if I'd kissed her? If she was true to Vincent I'd have to listen to some thrilling lecture about her loved one, and if she wasn't true to Vincent, well . . . then she wasn't the person I was starting to like.

She picked up her camera bag. "Want to walk up the road with me?" she asked almost shyly.

"I guess."

We didn't even speak for about five minutes, and then, since it was all I could think of, I asked about Vincent.

"How long have you known your boyfriend?"

"Who?"

"Vincent. Wasn't that his name?"

"Oh yeah. Vincent. Well, let's see. I've known Vincent all my life, I guess. You know, it's a small town."

I nodded. "When did you start dating him?"

"Um. Maybe two years ago, I guess."

"Wow. You've been going with him for two years already. That's pretty long."

"I guess so." She turned away to take a picture of some kids playing with a stick in the mud, but she didn't seem to really concentrate on it.

"And you love him? You think you'll stay together forever?"

"Well, I guess. I mean, we are pretty young still."

"But you love him?"

"I said I did, didn't I?" She got irritated so easily.

As we walked on I caught a glimpse of someone familiar standing near a raggedy old barn a little ways off the road. "Isn't that our illustrious guide?" I asked Cat.

"Yeah, it's Diego. Who's he talking to?"

"Can't see from here."

"Follow me." Cat crouched down behind a fence that ran beside the road and crawled along so she wouldn't be seen by Diego. I felt stupid following her, but what else could I do? If I kept standing he'd see me and then *she'd* look stupid.

"What are we doing this for?" I asked.

"I want to see what's going on."

"You are a snoop!"

"I'm just a curious person."

"Hah!" I snorted. "Don't you know what curiosity did to Cat?"

But she ignored me. When we got close enough we could see both men.

"It's the guy from the Research Station. Andre. The guy who helped Diego find the orphan tortoises," Cat said.

"Okay. Now we know. Let's get out of here before they see us."

"Wait!" Cat put her camera up to her face and began to focus.

"What are you doing?"

"I don't have a good picture of Diego. This will be great, with that old barn in the background. I can put it on telephoto . . ."

Diego turned around and looked right at us. "Hey! Who's there? Come out here!" He came running over to us while Andre melted away into the barn.

Cat and I stood up. "Hi." I said lamely, feeling like a total jerk.

"It's just us," Cat began. "I didn't mean to scare you. I like to take photographs when people don't know . . ."

"Why are you taking photographs of me? Did somebody send you out here? What are you doing way out here? All the tourists are in town!" Diego had grabbed hold of Cat's arm and was pulling at her.

"I know they are. I just wanted to walk in the countryside. Ow!"

"Let her go," I said. "We weren't doing anything."

He let go of Cat's arm, but he still looked furious. "Were you listening to our conversation?"

"No," Cat said. "Really. We just sneaked up so I could take a picture of you. I just wanted to take your picture." She looked close to tears by then, and I felt really terrible about the whole thing. Why was he freaking out about this? Cat was so embarrassed.

"I was having a private conversation," Diego said, trying to calm himself down. "I don't like people spying on me."

"We weren't spying," I said.

"Okay. I believe you. Next time don't scare people like that," he said, attempting a smile so we'd think he wasn't shaking in his booties.

"I'm really sorry," Cat said.

He waved us away. As we turned back down the road, Cat was trembling.

"God, I never thought he'd get so upset," she said.

"He was scared. That guy is up to something — I haven't trusted him since the beginning. He's always nervous. And then lying to Sofia last night. Something is going on with him."

Cat shook her head. "Some people just don't like to have their pictures taken," she said. "I should have asked him first."

"And do they usually grab your arm and twist it off? That guy Andre slipped away while Diego was yelling at us. I'm telling you, something weird is going on here."

"But Diego is so nice to everybody on the ship . . ."

"If this was anybody else, you'd be asking a hundred questions about it yourself. It's just because you've got a crush on Diego."

"I do not! Now you're yelling at me!"

I *was* yelling. Man, these days I got set off by the slightest thing. I felt like all my nerves were rubbed raw or something. The whole afternoon was one crazy thing after another. And then, when I turned to look at Cat, I saw she was walking along, quietly crying.

10/Cat

What a horrible day! I should have known in the morning when I missed that great shot of the vermilion flycatcher — it was not a good sign.

I did get some good shots up at the pit crater and then later on before my battery got low. And when Noah said he'd been looking for me, I thought maybe it was going to be a great day, a really *wonderful* day. He almost kissed me, I know he did. He came *that* close to it. I couldn't believe it was really going to happen, and I was right.

Then he started asking me all these questions about *Vincent.* I forgot I even told him that stupid lie about being in love with Vincent. Why did I do that? I never get away with a lie; I'm a terrible liar. But now, if I tell him the truth, he'll really think I'm an idiot.

I should just forget about Noah. After this trip I'll never see him again anyway. I'll remember him though.

I've never known a boy like him. Sure, he's "looking good," as Tomoko would say, but it's more than that. He thinks about things. You could trust a person like that.

A person who saw you make a fool of yourself sneaking up on somebody and then bawling about it afterwards. Diego was so mad, I felt awful. I mean, I liked him a lot. But Noah was right — nobody gets *that* mad at you for taking their picture. I've never been so embarrassed.

Poor Noah. He didn't know what to do. He handed me his handkerchief. I never met a guy who carried a handkerchief before.

"Did he hurt you?" Noah asked me.

I shook my head, even though my arm did feel a little sore. "I'm fine. Don't pay any attention to me." Like that was possible."

As we walked back to town Noah put his hand gently on my back and rubbed a little warm circle. It felt so good I wished he would put his arms all around me and let me sink in a few minutes. But he didn't. Instead he worked up several unlikely theories about what was going on with Diego — at least I thought they were unlikely at the time. Maybe he was a government spy, Noah said, or a criminal afraid I'd blow his cover, or a guy dodging his child-support payments. Of course Noah would think of that one.

"Not bad," I said. "Your imagination is definitely improving." I made a big effort to pull myself together and blew my nose in his handkerchief. And then I noticed we were about to be attacked by a four-foot torpedo by the name of Jeremy.

"Noah!" he shrieked, grabbing him around the waist

and knocking me out of the way. "I saw you from down there!" He pointed to the main street of town and his parents, who were panting towards our group. I tried to mop up my face a little better.

"Jeremy, I told you not to run off like that!" Mr. McNuff lectured.

"He saw his friend coming, didn't you?" Mrs. McNuff said, grinning.

"What's the matter with her?" Jeremy asked Noah, pointing to my no doubt red and blotchy face.

"Oh, um," Noah stammered, "Cat, ah, twisted her ankle. She stepped in a hole down the road."

Very good cover, I thought. Bravo, Noah.

"Oh, darling, you mustn't walk on it then!" Mrs. McNuff said. "Sit down right here. I'm a pediatrician. Let me take a look at it."

"It feels much better now. I think —"

"You don't want to take a chance, dear, especially when you have so much walking to do on the islands."

What choice did I have? I sat down right there, in the dirt by the side of the road near the chicken pen, site of the famous kiss I never got. I just hoped *my* parents didn't come along and hear the whole silly story too.

Mrs. McNuff, or, I should say, Dr. McNuff, twisted and pummeled my ankle. Does this hurt? Does that hurt? If I *had* sprained my ankle, I'd have been screaming by the time she finished. Finally I convinced her the pain had magically disappeared and she set me free. Meanwhile Noah had been coerced into riding Jeremy around on his shoulders while Mr. NcNuff turned his bored, glassy stare at the chickens.

"You're a very lucky girl, Cat," Dr. McNuff said gravely. "A sprained ankle can be a painful experience. If I were you I wouldn't walk on it any more than necessary today."

I assured her I intended to take the first panga back to the *Santiago* and remain sequestered in my cabin for as long as possible. You see, I thought I'd already had a bad day. I didn't know it could only get worse.

Dr. McNuff took the panga back to the boat with me, leaving Jeremy and Noah to babysit for her husband. She found my parents and told them I'd had this medical emergency. Then she arranged for me to have dinner brought to my cabin so I wouldn't have to walk to the dining room. I decided to go with the flow. I could use a sick day.

"You do look a little pale, hon," Mom said. Mom and Dad sat with me while I ate my dinner.

"I guess I'm just tired." I smiled bravely.

"An experience like that is draining," Dad said. "You should get to bed early."

"Maybe we should stay with you more on the islands. I know you like your independence, but maybe if we'd been there . . ."

"Mom!" Suddenly I was afraid. What if they spent the next week trailing after me, making sure I didn't fall down? I'd never even have another good talk with Noah, much less another chance at a kiss. "It's not a big deal! I mean, I wasn't alone. I was walking with Noah."

"Still. It's lucky Dr. McNuff came along when she did."

Yes, wasn't that lucky? "Still, you can't be with me

every second. I mean, you guys are both interested in the birds, and I'm taking pictures, and . . . well, we aren't looking for the same things!"

Mom smiled. "It's nice you have Noah."

"I don't *have* Noah, Mom. We just talk sometimes."

"I know," Mom said indulgently. God, sometimes she's such a *mother*.

They left then, so I could go to bed early, but, of course, I couldn't sleep. I tossed and turned for a while, then got up to read, but I felt so restless, like I couldn't make anything go right. I guess I dozed off, but then suddenly I was wide awake again, and I had the feeling I'd never be able to go back to sleep.

So I got up and got dressed. I put on a heavy sweater and thick socks and took my blanket along, thinking I'd go sit up on deck. Maybe I could nap a little bit up there and then watch the sun come up. Wouldn't that be a positive way to start a new day?

It must have been around two or three o'clock. There was no noise on the boat and only the lights at the stairways were turned on. I padded silently up to the dark top deck. But before I could settle into a chair, I heard voices, harsh whispers, drifting up as though from the lower deck.

Quietly, I leaned over the railing to listen. The voices seemed to be coming from the water now, or maybe from a panga tied at the loading dock at the back of the boat.

They were men, but they spoke too quietly for me to understand what they were saying. At first I wasn't even sure what language they were speaking, but then I realized it must be Spanish. There was a lot of grunting, like they were moving something heavy. I tried to see what it was, but my eyes weren't used to the dark yet.

There was one small light attached to a wall just below me at the top of the stairs that went down to the crew cabins, but both men had their heads down as they passed under it. All I could see were dark shapes. After a minute they came up again and struggled with something else. I had the feeling they were unloading things from a panga; I could hear water splashing down there. I strained my eyes to see the men when they passed under the light again.

For just a second I saw them both, their faces tight with the effort of carrying the weight. It was Andre, the researcher from the Darwin Station, and Diego. What could they be doing so late at night? I watched them repeat the maneuver another time, but still I couldn't make out what it was they were holding. Something big, though; something heavy.

They seemed to be more excited now; their voices were getting louder and they were hurrying. This time as they moved the object from the panga I leaned as far over the side as I dared and as they passed quickly beneath the light, I saw what they were carrying.

And that's when I knew that Noah was right. I had to tell him! We had to figure out what to do next!

For a minute I couldn't remember where his cabin was, but I made myself think back to the day I saw him coming out of it, almost late for the panga. It was an outside cabin, on the second deck. At least it was on the side of the boat away from the panga dock. Diego and Andre wouldn't hear me. I ran.

"Noah!" I whispered as loudly as I dared, then knocked on his door. I hoped I had the right cabin; I

was in such a state I might tell anyone who answered the door. "Noah!" I banged a little louder.

The door opened and Noah stood there, looking tousled and perplexed in a T-shirt and boxer shorts. "Cat? What's going on? It's the middle of the night!"

"I have to talk to you! Now! It's an emergency!"

"Henry's in here," he said, brushing his hair out of his eyes.

"Come out here with me! Please!"

"All right. Just a minute. It's cold out there." He closed the door partway and I stood waiting and shaking. He came out with a pair of jeans pulled on, a jacket over his shoulder and socks in his hand.

"Let me just pull these on," he said.

"No. Come on! We have to hurry! But be quiet." I tiptoed back down the second floor deck to the rear of the boat, hoping there would still be something to see, to prove to Noah. But the panga was gone, out of sight.

"It was right there." I pointed. "If I'd been on this deck I would have seen everything."

"What was right there?"

"The panga. And Andre. Oh, Noah, you were right about Diego — he's a criminal!"

"Cat, I think you had a bad dream or something . . ."

"No, it wasn't a dream! I was up on the top deck and I saw the men loading them onto the *Santiago*. Andre must have brought them out from the Darwin Station on a panga, and Diego was waiting for him."

"*What* did they bring out from the Darwin Station? You're not telling me anything!"

"The tortoises! The four orphan tortoises of Casanova

Island! They stole them and they're on this boat somewhere!"

I was starting to shake by the time I said it out loud, and I probably looked more than a little nuts. Noah put his arm around my shoulders, but I hardly felt it.

"Look, Cat, let's go inside somewhere and talk about this."

"My room. We can go there," I said, and led Noah quickly inside and down to my cabin.

He still had his arm around my shoulder when he sat down next to me on the bed. "Now tell me again what you think happened."

"I don't *think* it happened, Noah, I *know* it. I *saw* them. Remember how much Diego wanted Sofia to go to that party while he stayed here on the boat? Now we know why!"

"But did you actually *see* the tortoises?"

"I saw one of them, the last one. But they moved four things — they went in and out four times. And the one I saw was the right size, too. All the other tortoises at the center were either much smaller or else the really big, old ones. These tortoises were four years old; I'd bet my life on it."

Noah sighed. "Look, it's not that I don't believe you. But you've made up these stories before — you love making a big drama out of every situation."

I couldn't believe Noah wasn't going to believe me! "But you're the one who figured out that Diego was up to something! You said he was nervous and you didn't trust him. This afternoon you even said he might be a criminal!"

"Well, I was under your influence then!" Noah stood up and tried to pace around, except the cabin was too small to pace in. "I mean, why would Diego steal the tortoises he saved in the first place? What would he *do* with them?"

"I don't know. Maybe he's planning to sell them to somebody — a zoo or something!"

"But he'd never get away with it. He'd lose his job."

"He *is* getting away with it! Nobody saw them but me, and even *you* don't believe me, so who do you think will?" The tears were building up again, but I was too mad to let them fall now.

Noah sat down next to me again and picked up one of my hands.

"You saw Diego and Andre? Their faces?"

"Yes, when they passed under the light. It was them," I said decisively.

"They carried four things onto the boat?"

"Heavy things. They were grunting."

"You saw one of them and it was a tortoise."

"Yes, Noah. I know what I saw."

"Okay then," he said, looking right at me. "I believe you."

I couldn't help it; I started to bawl. So, of course, then Noah put his arms around me and held me and let me cry away like a little kid. I got his T-shirt soaking wet. It was what I wanted, but unfortunately I was too miserable to enjoy it properly. Sometime I'd like to try it on a better day.

11/Noah

What a night! It must have been five o'clock by the time I finally got Cat to calm down a little. She was exhausted by then, so she left a note on her parents' door saying her ankle had kept her awake during the night and she was going to skip the island visit this morning and try to sleep.

I had a feeling the fate of the stolen tortoises didn't bother her as much as the fact that Diego was not the great guy she'd imagined him to be; she liked thinking of him as the hero of the turtles. I almost didn't want to leave her alone, but I didn't want to run into her mom and dad as I was leaving her cabin first thing in the morning either.

Of course there was no chance *I* was going to get back to sleep. I sat up on deck and watched the sun come up — *felt* it come up, since the temperature rose right along with it. I kept thinking, why would Diego *do* something so crazy?

I couldn't concentrate on breakfast, I had so many thoughts running through my head. That French woman Cat knows sat down at my table and pointed out that I had a coffee cup full of corn flakes and a bowl full of toast.

"I see a young man whose mind is not on food," she said with a sly smile.

"Guess not," I admitted.

"Thinking of my little friend Cat perhaps. A charming young woman, don't you think?"

"Yeah, she's nice," I said. Didn't these old geezers

have anything better to do than try to pair off the un-married passengers?

She made a shooing motion with her hand. "Nice has nothing to do with it. She *sees* you, young man. I suppose you're too young to recognize it."

"I'm kind of tired this morning," I said. "I'm not seeing much of anything." Maybe she'd take the hint.

She did, thank God, stand up, coffee cup in hand, but then she raised her face and voice to the ceiling and called out, "Men! I will never understand them!" And *then* she finally walked away, leaving me to stare down a whole dining room full of people who wondered what I'd done to a woman old enough to be my mother.

Henry banged his coffee cup down next to me. Everybody had to be loud this morning. "Hey, pal, where'd you take off to in the middle of the night? Like I didn't know." A big smirk spread across his face.

"Henry, you *don't* know, so don't go jumping to conclusions."

"Right. Like you aren't hanging around that girl night and day now. I told you she was a good one."

"She's not a 'good one,' Henry. She's a nice person, okay? I like her. That's all. I won't even see her again after next week."

Henry shrugged. "You could if you wanted to. There are ways."

"So how's it going with you and Miyoko?" I asked, just to get him off my back.

He made a face and looked around the dining room. "I'm trying to cool things down a little with her. It's a problem, being locked up on this boat for two weeks. I mean, I like her, but there's no escape. Besides, you said it yourself, I'm like Dad. I'm not a one-woman man."

"Do you think that was stamped on your head at birth or something? 'Not A One-Woman Man.' Don't you think it's possible you might actually fall in love with somebody someday and *want* to stay with her forever?"

"My brother, the romantic."

"I mean it. I think Miyoko really likes you. Cat thinks so too. The way she looks at you is not just let's-have-a-good-time-while-it-lasts. I think she's serious," I told him.

"You think so? That's a scary thought." Henry chewed his toast thoughtfully for a minute. "Maybe I better stay away from her altogether."

"Why? You're a grown-up! Why can't you let yourself fall in love? You always pull back!"

"Keep your voice down, Noah, for God's sake. Look, it's not as easy as you think. Women . . . they *want* things from you."

"Like what?"

"Well, like commitment, like marriage, like . . . real stuff."

"Well, what's wrong with real stuff?" I sighed. "Sorry, Henry. I'm not saying you should marry Miyoko or anything. I just hate to see you thinking that Dad's got the right answer to this thing. Maybe Dad's never really been in love at all."

"Yeah, well, who knows?" Henry said, clapping me on the back. "But let's not waste any time worrying about Dad. He gets by. Listen, I'm gonna duck out before Miyoko comes over here. See ya later!"

It was a small and strangely quiet group on the panga.

The newlyweds weren't speaking at all. Henry was late enough showing up that he managed to be far away from Miyoko, who kept flashing him a stunningly sad look. Jeremy had a runny nose so his doctor-mother was staying on the *Santiago* with him this morning. Diego — the rat — stood quietly in the front of the boat, stifling one yawn after the other. And, of course, Cat wasn't there.

Except in a funny way, she was.

As soon as we got out of the panga on the beach, I noticed the iguanas — they were all over the rocks like shingles on a house. You didn't notice them until you got close; they were lying on top of each other. And they weren't all black like the iguanas we'd seen on other islands — they had red patches on their sides and green along their backs. Diego was explaining rather listlessly that Española was the only island on which we'd see this particular type of iguana, and immediately everybody pulled out a camera.

Damn! Cat was missing this!

"Henry!" I called, running after him as he plodded on ahead. "Did you bring a camera?"

"A camera? Yeah, yeah, there's one in the pack, I think." He laughed as he began to paw through the pack he'd carried all week. "Clara gave me her camera, but I haven't even taken it out. It's not my thing." He pulled out a small black machine and handed it over.

"How do I use it?"

"I think it's all automatic. Point and shoot. It's got film. How come all of a sudden you want pictures?"

I shrugged. "I liked those iguanas — the way they were crawling all over each other."

Henry shook his head and walked on. I noticed Miyoko was keeping her distance. She must have taken the hint. As soon as I looked at the iguanas through the viewfinder I could see what Cat meant. By putting a frame around the scene, you changed it. You left out the uninteresting parts. It made you think about what *was* interesting. Did you want to have their spiny backs standing out against the sand, or would you rather get them looking right at you? Just a few or a whole pack of them? Every decision had a reason behind it. I was controlling the outcome of the picture. I felt like I was organizing life, at least this small part of it.

It was amazing. When I finished with the iguanas, I took pictures of sea lions, then a few blue-footed boobies, of course, a Galápagos hawk, and then — oh, it wasn't fair that Cat was missing this! — the albatrosses.

I'd always thought of albatrosses as big, clumsy birds that cause people bad luck. But these birds were beautiful. They had long, curving yellow beaks and downy, white heads and necks that looked regal. Diego pointed out a pair close to us that was involved in an elaborate ritual of sword-fighting with their beaks, beating out a rhythmic music.

"That is the mating ritual of the waved albatross. These two will mate for life. When the season is over, they might fly far across the world, but next year they will find this same small island again, and each other."

I took pictures. I took so many pictures I had to get more film from Henry. I took so many pictures, Diego yelled at me to catch up with the group, but I certainly didn't intend to let that liar tell me what to do. I was taking pictures for Cat; even though mine wouldn't be nearly as good as anything she could take, still she'd have pictures of albatrosses, mating for life.

By the time we got back to the *Santiago*, I was worn out. I grabbed a bite of lunch and went back to my cabin to sack out. There was a group going out snorkeling again, but I could skip that.

When I heard the knock on my door I jumped up, knowing who it would be.

"Hi," she said. "Were you sleeping?"

"It's okay. Come on in."

"Did you go to Española this morning?" she asked, perching on the end of Henry's bed.

"I did. I took pictures for you." God, I seemed to be blushing or something. I never blushed.

"You did? What did you take?"

"There were these birds, the waved albatrosses —"

"Oh, I missed the albatrosses! What were they like?" She put her hand on my knee, but she was listening to me so closely I don't think she even realized it was there. I did.

"They were the most beautiful birds I've ever seen. Big and white and soft-looking, with curving yellow beaks. They were all arranged in pairs like salt and pepper shakers or something. I felt like I was seeing things people never see. How the world all works, you know?"

She nodded. "Like you're one of the first people on earth. I've felt that all week."

"I wanted to take good pictures for you, but I know they won't be nearly as good as yours would have been."

She smiled, but there was something else pushing the albatrosses out of her mind. "Noah, I've got a plan. It's not much, but it's the only thing I can think of to do."

"What?"

She opened her belt pack and pulled out a veritable salad: lettuce, carrots, celery, radishes. "I asked Mom to bring me lunch in my room again. I know tortoises eat cactus, but where was I going to get cactus? So I thought tonight, when everybody's at dinner, we'll sneak down into the crew quarters and stick a little bit of food in front of each door. It might not work, but maybe we can hear where he's keeping them."

"Okay. But what good will that do?"

She looked steadily into my eyes. "You'll know I'm not crazy, that's what good it will do."

"Cat, I already said I believed you."

"I know you said it. And I appreciate that, but I want you to really know it. Okay?"

How could I say no? So at seven o'clock, we waited near the stairway that came up from the crew quarters, pretending to be discussing the intricacies of the Janus XR15. The captain was already in the dining room and so was Esther, who ran the gift shop. George and Annie came up the stairs together. Then Sofia emerged, her dark eyes throwing flames as usual.

Cat stepped in front of her. "Excuse me. We had a question about the giant tortoises, and I wondered if you could answer it?" This was not on the planned agenda. You never knew what was going to pop into Cat's head.

"If I can, certainly." She didn't smile.

"We were wondering if there are any tortoises in zoos anywhere. I mean, could Galápagos tortoises be sold to zoos?"

"No!" Sofia snapped. "These animals are protected

now. Finally. There was a time when they were sold to zoos, but that time is over. We let no tortoises leave these islands."

You felt like the enemy when Sofia turned that look on you. But I didn't really blame her. Her job was to protect the islands, but then she had to lead groups of silly tourists around all day who'd probably eat tortoise eggs themselves if you didn't tell them not to.

"Well, she doesn't know," I said, as Sofia stomped off. "I'll bet he isn't letting her in his room."

"I'll bet she doesn't even *want* to go in his room. She's not the forgiving type. And when she finds out he's selling tortoises to zoos, she'll probably murder him."

"We don't know that for sure," I pointed out.

"What else could he be doing with them?" Cat asked. I had no answer.

After another five minutes, Diego appeared, looking a bit rumpled in his white dinner uniform. He nodded to us, and I smiled back, like a good spy, but Cat could only just manage not to spit at him. As soon as he was out of sight, we dashed down the stairs. There were six doors, and six people had gone in to dinner, so we felt pretty safe. The panga drivers' rooms were on the other side of the boat.

We started at the first door, putting some pieces of lettuce and carrot down and sliding them partway under. Then we listened. Not a sound. I wished I knew what we were listening for — these tortoises were pretty silent animals, it seemed to me. Maybe we wouldn't hear anything. Maybe they hated carrots and celery.

I took the pack and went down the line, pushing vegetables underneath each door. It occurred to me we were going to be hard-pressed to explain this behavior if anyone came down the stairs. After the food was distributed, we moved from door to door, listening. Nothing.

"Cat, I don't think they make any noise," I said. "You don't have to prove this to me."

"I just want to hear *something*. They must make some kind of noise. You'd think we'd at least hear them walking around in there," she said.

"Wait a minute! I just remembered something!" I sat back on my heels, amazed at myself. "Remember what Diego said about the pirates and whalers?"

"Sure. He said they destroyed the tortoise population by taking huge numbers of them on their boats for food. What's that got to do with —"

"And the way they stored all that live meat until they were ready to use it was . . ." I waited for her to get it.

"On their backs!" She stared at me. "You're a genius! I thought you weren't even listening to Diego's lectures?"

I shrugged. "I guess more stuff got through than I thought. I had an image of hundreds of these big creatures stacked up on their backs — it was hard to forget."

"Of course that's what Diego would do too. He wouldn't want them walking all over his room."

It was right then we heard the noise, like a low, slow drumbeat, the sound of something kicking steadily against the wall. We pressed our ears up to the door we were standing in front of. Sure enough. We were definitely hearing *something*.

"They're in there, all right," I said. "But what kind of noise is that?"

"One of them is trying to turn over," Cat said, her fingers arching like claws against the door.

I nodded silently, realizing that Cat had been right. I'd *wanted* to believe her, but I hadn't really been able to. Of course I didn't have to admit it to her, but I felt like a creep anyway.

"Maybe it hears us. Maybe it's trying so hard because it's afraid. We ought to go," Cat said. "The poor thing doesn't know who's a friend and who's an enemy."

We walked back up to the dining room without saying another word. I don't know about Cat, but I kept seeing that poor guy thrashing around helplessly, hoping he'd be able to flip his bulk over and lumber off. We missed the first course, but we assured everyone we weren't hungry for salad anyway.

12/Cat

Everybody was all excited this morning because we were anchored off Floreana Island for two days. I guess the snorkeling is supposed to be especially good there; Henry got a group of people all excited about it and Diego agreed it was the thing to do this morning.

And then Mr. Baumgartner had been telling everybody about his father's journal and the woman, Jacqueline Marche, who lived with his father sixty years ago on this island. The Baumgartners planned to go looking for her, with Annie as their guide, and I thought I'd go with them. It was such a romantic story and kind of a mystery besides — just what I needed this morning.

But I also wanted to put some distance between Noah and me. Yesterday had been confusing in more ways than one. Noah was suddenly being very nice to me, and I didn't know why. Did he just feel sorry for me because I kept blundering into these situations I couldn't handle? Maybe he still thought I was a silly hick. I knew I wasn't much like the girls he dated at home. Although he never mentioned having a girlfriend, I imagined him hanging around on a yacht with a girl in a string bikini.

Of course he sat down with me at breakfast. "So, what should we do about it?" he said, before he'd even shoveled the sugar into his thick coffee.

"Do? What do you mean?"

"About the tortoises," he whispered. "We should tell the captain or somebody."

"The captain?" I laughed. "What makes you think he'd believe us? Besides, I don't think he's like a real ship's captain. He's just somebody who can think fast in three languages, and comfort the seasick. I don't think he'd be much good in a crisis."

"Well, we have to do *something,* don't we?"

"Not this minute. We'll keep an eye on him, see if we can figure anything out," I said, picking around in my bran flakes.

"I don't know about you, but I don't have much experience with detective work." He sighed. "I keep thinking there must be some rational explanation for it."

"If there was a rational explanation, would he be *sneak-*

ing them onto the ship? I don't think so." I slammed my chair back as if I were angry. "I've got stuff to do in my cabin before we leave. I'll see you."

Noah looked up, surprised. I couldn't imagine what he thought of me now. The problem was, I was having incredibly strong feelings about Noah. When he rubbed my back, when he took my hand, when he put his arms around me in the cabin, I wasn't just crying about what I was *crying* about — Diego or tortoises or whatever — I was also crying because I didn't want it to end, I didn't want Noah to get up and leave me, I didn't want the trip to be over without at least one kiss from him. And I couldn't stand the idea of never seeing him again. I mean, I felt like I felt about Vincent, only magnified about a hundred times.

There was a way Noah smiled at me where the smile wasn't just curling up his mouth, but seemed to be coming out of his eyes too, that made everything feel loose inside my body, like there was hot lava running in my veins and heating up all my muscles. I wished there was a Loveometer you could measure your feelings on, so you could be sure of what you felt.

One thing I know is that when people give hearts for Valentine's Day and talk about being heartbroken, it's not just some poetic idea. Because you do feel it in your heart, the I-love-you and the Why-don't-you-love-me; both of them are alive and well in that one hard-working organ. I imagined it like a sponge, soaking up every word and smile, then getting so soppy with emotion it leaks out all over the place.

Ugh, it was just too pathetic to be sixteen and pining for somebody who didn't feel the same way. Therefore,

I decided to stay away from Noah as much as possible, figuring that was the way to get over this thing. But when we got to Floreana, it turned out he'd planned to go with the Baumgartners too.

"I thought you and Henry were supposed to be testing some snorkeling equipment," I said.

He shook his head. "Not me. That's Henry's assignment. Dad's probably going to offer Henry a job with the company. He ought to. Henry's practically a poster boy for Snowbird."

"But you're not."

"I could have been. I don't know what I am anymore."

Oh god, don't get that sad look on your face, Noah. Are you trying to kill me?

"Look at Henry," he said, shaking his head. "What an idiot! He's making up to that newlywed woman now, what's her name?"

"Kathy Fogarty? He's hitting on her now?"

"It sure looks like it. I don't see her husband. He must not have come this morning."

"Poor Miyoko," I said, knowing how she must feel.

"At least she's going snorkeling too. She must have rented equipment on the boat."

"I didn't think she knew how to snorkle. I thought Henry was teaching her."

Noah shrugged. "It's not hard to learn. She's a good swimmer."

"Let's go! This vay to Madame Marche's house!" Mr. Baumgartner shouted.

It was a small group that headed out over the rocks: the Baumgartners, Monique LaFarge and her no-longer-sick sister Yvonne, and Noah and me. I knew Monique wouldn't be able to resist meeting a beautiful French woman with a mysterious past.

"Diego said she owns a tea shop," Yvonne said. "Won't that be lovely? Tea on a wild, deserted island!"

"Darling, forty people live on this deserted island," Monique said.

Yvonne ignored her. "I hope they have lemons way out here. I abhor tea without lemon. At least we can get out of the sun for a while." She yanked her hat down over her eyes.

Monique glowered at her. "You should have stayed on the ship if you didn't want sun in your eyes."

"The ship? The ship rocks like a constant earthquake. I'm sick of the ship!"

"And the ship is probably sick of you, too." Monique made a clicking sound with her tongue. "I can see now why you've had three husbands. Who can stand the complaining?"

Yvonne narrowed her eyes at her sister. "And I see also why *you've* never married at all! You are so unsympathetic."

"The man I marry will not need sympathy. He will be a lover of life!"

"The man you want to marry only exists in a book!"

They continued to battle their way up the sandy trail through the delicate Palo Santo trees, but Noah and I dropped back so we didn't have to listen. I imagined how much Jacqueline Marche must look forward to having the tourists come and visit her. Not much like her rich yachting friends of the thirties.

"Madame Marche's house is just the other side of those

trees," Annie said. We walked a few more minutes until we saw the small house surrounded by flowers.

"That's it!" Mrs. Baumgartner shouted. "I recognize it from photographs!"

All of a sudden I felt wrong, busting in on somebody I didn't even know with this noisy group. Was this woman another sea lion or a rare bird we wanted to put on our lists? I hung back as the Baumgartners raced up the path to the house, followed by Annie, Monique, and Yvonne.

Noah started after them, then turned around. "What's the matter?"

"I don't know. I feel like we're invading her or something. I wish we at least had something to give her."

Noah looked around, thinking. But all we had with us were our hats and cameras — Noah's been taking pictures lately too.

He shrugged. "Not a shell or a feather or a rock. Nothing to offer but our sparkling personalities."

A small, white-haired woman had emerged from the house and spoke German to the Baumgartners. I would have turned around to leave, but she began to motion to all of us saying, "Kommen Sie herein, bitte!"

The Baumgartners must have told her we weren't German, so she switched to English. "Come, come. You must have some tea!" Another one of those people who can talk to everybody.

I walked to the doorway, just to look inside and listen to a little of the conversation. Her home was tiny, with just the essentials inside, a table, a cabinet, some chairs, a bed. No refrigerator, no television, nothing electric.

But it was beautiful, with lace curtains hanging in the windows.

"Was it this house," Mr. Baumgartner asked, "that my father helped build?" He must have already introduced himself in those first minutes.

Jacqueline Marche smiled warmly. She was small, and quite old, her skin brown and wrinkled, the colors of her dress all bleached out. I tried to imagine what she must have looked like when she was young and beautiful, but I couldn't. It's hard to imagine that old people were ever really young.

"Hans Baumgartner's son. I can hardly believe it. So many years ago." She stared out the window a minute as if she was looking back at those days. "But no, it was not this house your father built. My son helped me to build this one after my husband died. The old one couldn't last. Nothing lasts long in this hard climate. Nothing but me," she said with a laugh.

Monique spoke to her in French then, while Yvonne picked through the tea choices. I could tell Mr. Baumgartner was annoyed. He couldn't understand what they were saying, and he was probably anxious to get back to the story of his father. After all, that was why they'd come. I thought we should all leave them alone so he could find out, but it looked like Monique and Yvonne were settling in.

Madame Marche noticed Noah and me standing just inside the door. "Won't you come in and have some tea?"

"No! No, thank you, Madame Marche," I said. "I'm not thirsty. I think I'll walk back to the beach and take a swim."

Noah looked at me like I'd lost my mind. "You don't swim."

"You can stay, Noah. I just want to go back now."

Jacqueline Marche took my hand in her tiny one. "It's nice to be free in the Galápagos, isn't it?"

"Thank you," I said stupidly, heading out the door. I wanted to turn around and yell to her, "Are you free? Are we ruining everything for you or saving it?"

"Stay on the trail!" Annie called after me.

"Wait a minute. You're not leaving me with this bunch of old ladies." Noah was beside me.

"I thought you wanted to take a picture of her? Look around the place?"

"Well, I did, but if you're not going to . . . I mean, my pictures aren't going to be any good anyway."

I sighed. "She would have been a great subject."

"Well, go back and take pictures then. What's with you today?"

I didn't know exactly. "I feel like I'm stealing something from her," I said. "It just doesn't seem polite to sit and gawk at her. She's not a blue-footed booby."

"The question is, is it polite to gawk at the blue-footed booby?"

I sighed. "I need to sit down a minute," I said, dropping down on a large stone. "I'm hot."

Noah didn't sit but paced a little, the way he does. "You're still upset about the Diego thing, aren't you?"

I nodded. It wasn't a lie; I was upset about that. Not *only* that, however.

"Look, so the guy's a creep. In another week you'll never see him again."

121

This line of reasoning was not helping me. "Noah, I really liked Diego. We had dinner with him the second night on board and he seemed like a good person. I mean, I always thought I could tell about people . . ."

"How can you tell if somebody is 'a good person' over dinner? It seems to me it's impossible to know anything about anybody ever. People are too complicated." Noah was digging in the dirt with a stick. "And they always let you down in the end."

"That's a terrible thing to say," I said, taking it very personally.

He shrugged. "It's been my experience."

"You're only sixteen! How much experience do you have!"

"Enough, okay?"

"Just because your parents are getting a divorce doesn't mean that all people —"

"I don't want to talk about my parents."

"That *is* what you're talking about! That's what you *always* talk about, whether you know it or not!"

That got under his skin. "I don't need any amateur psychiatry, Cat. I'm sure my father will be happy to pay for the best shrink in Boston."

"For many years, I hope. Because you sure need it!" It was giving me a really nasty thrill to be mean to Noah. I knew I was hurting him but I couldn't stop. As soon as he stomped away I felt truly sorry about it. Maybe he was right about people letting each other down. First I was thinking I loved him, then I was saying awful things to him.

I followed him back to the snorkeling beach, but kept

well behind. I didn't feel like apologizing right now. It seemed like he'd hurt my feelings, too.

Noah came into the clearing at the beach before I did, and I saw him stop for a minute, as if he was looking at something. Then he started to run, fast. I walked faster to see what was happening. There was a man running out into the water toward Diego . . . but what was Diego doing? He seemed to be . . . he was dragging something out of the water. And there was Miyoko behind him. Oh god.

Diego was dragging a body. And the body was Henry.

By the time Noah and I got there Diego had Henry laid out on his back and was giving him mouth-to-mouth resuscitation. The only sounds were the man who'd helped Diego bring Henry to shore telling everybody to move back and give him some room, and Kathy Fogarty's little gasping cries. Even Noah just stood quietly and stared.

It seemed like an eternity, but it was probably only a minute or two before Henry choked and coughed and turned over on his stomach to throw up several gallons of the Pacific Ocean.

Then Noah started screaming. "What happened? What the hell happened?"

People came up to Diego to shake his hand, but he waved them away so he could get his walkie-talkie and call to the *Santiago* to have them send a panga out for Henry. How confusing. Now I guessed Diego must be a hero — he'd saved Henry's life!

Wrong again. As soon as he was off the walkie-talkie, Diego began an explanation.

"I only pulled him the last few meters. She's your hero — over there!" He pointed to Miyoko, who was squatting in the sand next to the still-retching Henry. "I need some towels now. I want to keep him covered until the panga comes. He's very cold."

In fact, Henry was shivering significantly. Noah helped him sit up, then collected towels from people and draped them around his brother. Miyoko curled up next to him, her arms around his waist, warming him her own way. It almost seemed too private to see.

"But what happened?" Noah kept asking. "Henry's a terrific swimmer."

Diego shook his head. "I told everyone to stay on this side of the rocks. Most people don't go out that far anyway. If you go out too far on the other side of those rocks, there's a tidal current. It's very strong — you can't swim against it."

"Henry not meaning to go there," Miyoko said, looking up with tears in her eyes.

"Maybe it's my fault," Kathy Fogarty said timidly. "He was showing me how the snorkel works and all, and I asked him how far out you can go with those things. So he went far out there . . . I thought he knew what he was doing!"

"I . . . I couldn't get back in," Henry panted, then lay back in the sand.

"Did you see him go out, Miyoko?" Noah asked. "How did you get him out of the current?"

Miyoko sat in the sand now, Henry hanging on to her hand. "I see Henry go out snorkeling with girl. Henry like show offing for girls. I stay watching, not go too close. I see Henry going where Diego say not, so I go too."

"You could have drowned too!" I said.

"I watch Henry," she said simply.

"But you're so small, Miyoko," Noah said. "How could you save Henry?"

"I don't know," she said quietly. "I be strong. Henry trying to swim in. I swim him out of current first, then bring in. I learn swim good too."

"That's for sure," Diego said, beginning to relax, now that it looked as though everybody was all right. The panga arrived and Noah and Diego helped Henry in. Miyoko went along, sitting on the floor of the panga with Henry's head in her lap.

As soon as the panga left, the tension broke, and people began to talk loudly and laugh and generally feel good to be alive, I guess. But I kept standing there, watching the panga get smaller and smaller. How could I ever be mean to Noah? I was in awe of Miyoko; she was completely true to her own feelings, whatever the return on her investment might be.

I kept hearing her quiet voice saying, "I watch Henry. I be strong."

13/Noah

I thought, My brother's dead. I was just starting to like the guy and now he's gone. I watched Diego drag him up the beach and I wished I had another chance . . . and then I got one.

Thank god for Miyoko. I still can't believe a small person like her could have saved a huge guy like Henry, but Diego said you never know what kind of strength you have until it's tested. And apparently Miyoko didn't panic; she realized she'd have to get him out of the current first and then swim in to shore.

Henry kept saying how he felt like a damned fool, but Diego told him he wasn't the first person to find out that a beautiful ocean could also be cruel.

"With all his boats and snorkels and diving equipment, man starts to think he can be in charge of the ocean. Now you'll have a healthy respect for it. Yes?" Just the way he spoke calmed us all down. Maybe there *was* some explanation for him stealing the tortoises. How could a person like this be a criminal?

While I helped Henry take a shower — he was so wiped out he could hardly stand up — Miyoko must have taken one also. By the time I got him in a pair of pajamas, Miyoko, Captain Bolmeier, and the ship's doctor were all standing in the doorway waiting to get their hands on him. The captain kept expressing his "regret at the incident," but he also kept pointing out that Henry had been warned not to swim beyond the rocks. Like he was afraid we were going to sue him because Henry couldn't follow directions. He was really ticking me off.

The doctor checked Henry over pretty thoroughly and pronounced him well but exhausted, prescribing only sleep as a cure. Once they'd gone Miyoko was left standing there alone in the doorway, staring at Henry as though she could hardly bear the distance between them. Henry held out his arms. "Hey," he whispered hoarsely. "I hear you saved my life."

Miyoko, who must have been worn to a frazzle herself, ran to him and buried her face in his chest.

The Henry I knew would have looked at me over her shoulder and winked. Another dame in love with Henry the Third. But that isn't what happened. He just held her, very tightly, so tightly I began to fear for her ability to breathe. But Miyoko didn't seem to mind.

I whispered, "Henry, the doctor said you're supposed to sleep."

Henry nodded, but his eyes remained closed. I shut the door behind me when I left.

Dinner had already started, and since I had nowhere else to go, I wandered in, unaware that Henry's near-death experience had made me a semicelebrity. From all sides people were coming up to ask how he was, even Kathy Fogarty and her husband Brian, who were arm in arm and seemed finally to have patched up their spat. The Baumgartners, who had missed the whole event, pulled me down at their table and questioned me like police officers.

Yes, it was his own fault. Yes, Diego had told him about the rocks. No, no one but Miyoko had seen him get in trouble. Yes, she had risked her life. No, she wasn't hurt.

Once I had drawn the event vividly enough for them

to picture the whole thing, they turned to telling the story of their afternoon with Jacqueline Marche.

"She knew a man I never met," Mr. Baumgartner said sadly. "A fearless sailor, a skilled carpenter, and a hardworking farmer. Madame Marche said with one old donkey and a homemade plow he turned over acres of land. A boat brought seeds from the mainland. They planted onions and root vegetables and even fruit trees." He shook his head. "The man I knew collected stamps."

"You'd think you'd know something that important about your own father," I said, then stopped, realizing there was plenty I didn't know about mine either.

"People put the past behind them, I suppose," Mr. Baumgartner said, and I shivered thinking about it.

"Why did he leave the island?" I asked.

"Apparently they had a fight. It sounds like men were falling in love with her all the time!" Mr. Baumgartner chuckled.

"And she with them!" Mrs. Baumgartner put in.

"My father got tired of it, I suppose. He wanted a woman all to himself. But it must have been quite a life for a while."

"*If* you can believe all she says," Mrs. Baumgartner said. "She's an old woman now. She may embroider her life as she looks back on it. Or at least remember it her own way."

Mr. Baumgartner nodded in agreement. I thought of my mother making sense of her life by blaming men for her troubles. I wondered if Evelyn and Clara found different ways.

I regretted not staying to hear Madame Marche's stories. Of course, if I had, I wouldn't have arrived back on the beach just as Henry was being dragged out of the water. I also wouldn't have had the pleasure of Cat screaming at me about how screwed up she thought I was.

I sneaked a look around the dining room to see where Cat might be, but couldn't find her. She must have left already. With all the confusion in the afternoon, I'd almost forgotten about Cat getting so mad at me. Not that it was the first time a girl ever yelled at me or anything, but it was the first time I couldn't shrug it off.

Cat didn't play the kinds of games most girls played with guys. She just said what she thought and I liked her for that. I thought I could trust her.

And then she told me she thought I was cuckoo over my parents' divorce — I didn't expect that from her. When was I going to learn? Everybody hurts you sooner or later.

When I finally left the Baumgartners, I wasn't sure where to go. Would Miyoko still be with Henry? I stood on the deck in front of our cabin door, looking over the railing. The moon was almost full and spread a carpet of light over the black ocean. So much had happened it seemed I must have been on this boat for months, not just days.

I heard somebody walking toward me . . . it's funny how I almost expected her.

"Hi," Cat said cautiously, leaning on the railing next to me.

"Hi," I answered.

"How's Henry? Is he all right?"

"Yeah. The doctor checked him. He's fine."

"Good." She stopped talking and I half expected her

to walk away again. Finally she said, "You know, that first night, when you and Henry sat down at our table in the dining room? I wasn't too crazy about Henry. He seemed so full of himself."

"He is full of himself."

"I know. But now I like him anyway. He has another side. He's not the person he sounds like at first."

How did she know something like that about my brother when I'd only just discovered it myself? "What did you think of *me* that first night? Did you think I was crazy right away?" I was hurt, but I sounded angry.

Cat was quiet for a long time. My heart beat so hard I was afraid it was doing internal damage to some other organs. Finally she put one hand tentatively on my arm.

"I'm sorry I said that, Noah. I didn't mean it. It's just that you hurt my feelings . . ."

"I hurt *your* feelings?"

"Yes! When you said people always let you down! *I* don't let people down."

"You don't, huh? Well, that Vincent's a lucky guy, I guess."

Cat snatched her fingers off my arm like it was a hot stove. "How come you're so interested in Vincent all the time?"

"I'm not. You're the one who mentioned him in the first place. Your one true love, I believe you said."

"Right." She spun away from me. "See you later."

"Wait a minute!" Damn. Cat was trying to patch up our argument and I was making it worse. "You didn't answer my question. What did you think of me that first night at dinner?"

Cat gave the question her usual thoughtful consideration, then said, "I thought you were the one person on this boat I wanted to get to know."

God, sometimes she just blew me away with the truth. And then she disappeared before I had a chance to react. I considered following her to her cabin, but what was the point? She had this boyfriend and everything . . . it would be too confusing.

But when I opened the door to my cabin, Miyoko and Henry were in there, curled up together, fast asleep. I didn't think I could stand to sleep in the same room with *that*, especially if Henry woke up in the morning and threw her out, so I took a pillow, a couple of blankets, and a sweater to survive the night out on deck.

Actually, it was a terrific night. The sky was full of stars again, and the water lapped peacefully around the boat. I positioned my deck chair so I had a good view of Floreana, island of flowers, where Jacqueline Marche and Hans Baumgartner were once young lovers. There was a large hill in the middle of the island, and in the moonlight the lacy, spindly trees that covered it looked like fine silver webs tying the whole thing up. I intended to keep my eyes on that hill until the sun came up, but after the excitement of the day, I must have fallen asleep right away.

But I did manage to see the sun come up. Just as the first bright rays were shooting out over the Pacific Ocean, my brother pulled a chair up next to mine.

"Noah, I want to talk to you. Wake up, Noah!" He was jiggling the chair and I really had no choice.

"How you doing? You okay?" I murmured, pulling my blanket up and snuggling in for a last glimpse of my dream. Cat was in it and I didn't feel like letting go of it yet. I was in the water and Cat was pulling me out the way Diego had pulled Henry out. But I wasn't exactly drowning because the water was really . . . flowers? Something like that.

"Listen, Bud, wake up. I need to talk to you."

"Okay," I said, rubbing my eyes. "I'm awake. How are you? I bet you're sore today."

"A little, yeah. That's not the problem, though." Now I noticed that Henry was frowning, rubbing a hand up and down his forehead.

"You feel sick? Maybe we should get the doctor —"

"No, no, I'm not sick. I'm fine. It's just . . . I mean, you don't have something like that happen to you every day, Noah. It makes you think, you know?"

"Yeah, I guess so."

"I mean, when I started to go under yesterday, when I knew I didn't have the strength to swim back to shore, I suddenly thought, oh god, that's all there was to it! I saw what a waste my life was."

I put my hand on Henry's shoulder. "Your life isn't a waste. Jeez, you're just starting your life — how could it be a waste?"

But Henry shook his head. "I feel so confused now. She risked her life to save me, did you know that?"

"I heard, yeah."

"Why would anybody do that?"

I knew Henry had the same answer to that question I did, but I didn't plan on saying it out loud.

"I mean, how am I supposed to feel now? When somebody does something like that?"

"How *do* you feel?"

"I don't know!" Henry banged his fist on the chair

arm. "I'm grateful to her, of course, but that doesn't seem to be enough."

"Look, Henry, you can't pretend you're in love with her just because she saved your life."

"Maybe I wouldn't be pretending." Henry stuck the heels of his hands into his eyes and pushed them around like he was trying to blind himself. "I don't know what I feel. I woke up this morning with Miyoko lying there in my arms and for the first time in my life I felt completely happy and peaceful. I'll tell you — at first I wasn't sure if I was really awake, or if I was dead, or what. And then I remembered the whole thing, yesterday and before that, and I just freaked out. I jumped up and ran. I feel like I don't know what I'm doing."

"Henry, you had a really traumatic experience yesterday. It's bound to affect you for awhile. Try to calm down a little. If I know Miyoko, she won't make any demands on you."

"Maybe she ought to. I wish she would. I wish she'd yell at me or beat me up or something."

"What?"

"What's the matter with me, Noah? I'm scared to death!"

14/Cat

There were only five days left on the trip. I was going to tell Noah I made up the thing about Vincent. What could I lose? If he thought I was a jerk, well, it would be a bad five days, but at least I'd see how things stood without that lie between us.

All night I'd been dreaming of Miyoko and hearing her quiet, lilting voice say, "I watch Henry. I be strong." In my dream I saw her saving Henry, carrying him in her arms, which of course she'd never really be able to do, then giving him mouth-to-mouth resuscitation, which looked more like French kissing than lifesaving. And then all of a sudden Henry and Miyoko turned into Noah and me, just as Captain Bolmeier came screaming over the intercom with his salute to morning. That guy's really starting to get to me.

I was nervous as we lined up for the panga ride back to Floreana, but not as nervous as Diego.

"If we are lucky today we'll be seeing the flamingos performing their mating ritual at the lagoon near Punta Cormoran. This is an experience you won't forget." Meanwhile the guy looked so uptight he could hardly force the words out of his mouth. He kept tucking in his shirt and smoothing down his hair like his hands were incapable of rest.

Sofia was standing across the deck talking to some Dolphins and Diego kept shooting glances in her direction. Finally she walked right past him, head up, and said nothing. Diego looked a little sick, but he was silent.

"She's mad at him and she doesn't even know what he's done," Noah said, coming up behind me.

"He looks awfully guilty today," I said.

"Maybe he is doing something legal with the tortoises," Noah whispered. He leaned so close I could feel his breath on my face. It made the roots of my hair tingle.

134

"If it was legal, he wouldn't have to do it in the middle of the night," I said, trying not to sound breathless. "But don't worry, I'm keeping my eye on him."

"*You're* keeping an eye on him? You think you're Nancy Drew? Maybe we ought to tell somebody else."

"Noah! Not yet! I don't want to get Diego in trouble if he isn't doing anything wrong."

"You just said he was!"

"Just please let me do this myself."

"I thought I was in on it, too." Noah sounded disappointed.

"You are. You are in on it." God, it was hard not to let it show how much I liked this guy.

We boarded the panga and then watched as Henry followed Miyoko down the stairs. They both looked pale and a little shaky. They didn't speak to each other or anybody else, but sat together quietly.

"How's Henry today?" I asked Noah. "He doesn't look so hot."

"I don't know. He's kind of confused. About Miyoko and everything. Why she risked her life."

"He doesn't know?"

"Well, I think he does, but he's not sure how to feel about it."

"Poor Miyoko!"

"How come the girl always gets the sympathy?" Noah said, annoyed. "Henry's having a hard time with this, too."

"I know. I just meant, poor everybody." What I *really* meant was, poor me, who has to get up the nerve to tell Noah the truth, or regret it forever.

Another wet landing. As we sat around drying our feet

135

so we could put our sneakers back on, I realized the group had settled into a certain camaraderie. We'd gotten over being thrown together in this unusual stewpot, and had decided to make the best of it. Kathy and Brian Fogarty, bless their hearts, had made friends with Jeremy. Watching them grin at each other over his head as they walked hand in hand, I wondered if their arguments had to do with having kids. The elderly couple had befriended Sachiko and Tamoko; I heard them inviting the girls to stop in Toronto before heading back to Japan. And Mom and Dad — the loners of Benson River — were avidly describing other birding adventures they'd experienced to Dr. and Mr. McNuff, who'd relaxed once they got Jeremy out of their hair.

It was a pleasant group now, except for Diego, who plodded around nervously in his bare feet waiting for the rest of us.

"Ah, we are in luck today," Diego said without enthusiasm once we reached the lagoon. "The flamingos are headed toward us. Watch how they advance. The males are all in a pack, the ones with their necks extended."

Everybody laughed at the noise they made, a kind of squawking bark. They looked ridiculous, walking first in one direction, then turning, all fifteen or twenty of them at the same time, and walking in the other direction.

"Is this the flamingo equivalent of cruising for chicks?" Brian Fogarty asked.

"Not exactly," Diego explained. "The males are showing off, hoping to be chosen. But they don't do the choosing; the females do."

"Gloria Steinem helped get that written into their constitution!" I thought surely we'd heard all the jokes we needed to about human behavior being just like the birds', especially if it made women look bossy, but apparently Brian still had one left in him. I was glad to see at least it wasn't Henry making dumb jokes anymore.

The birds were coming in close and I got a half-dozen shots I thought might actually be great. I noticed Noah was also taking pictures, with that automatic camera his brother gave him.

"If you really like taking pictures, I'll show you how to use the Janus," I offered. "The results are much better."

I gave him a quick rundown on f-stops and apertures and let him take a few shots.

"There's lots to learn about photography, but the basics are easy."

"I'm surprised how much fun this is. Maybe when I get home I'll get a decent camera and take a course or something."

How could he just say it like that: *when I get home.* Like it was no big deal that in mere days we'd never set eyes on each other again. I couldn't stop thinking about it and it was making me really grumpy.

"Okay. When you've got enough pictures, we're going down this trail. We'll meet at a lovely white sand beach where you can take a swim if you'd like." Diego headed up the trail followed by most of the group.

I put down my camera. "These guys are really stupid-looking."

Noah smiled. "I've never known you to be judgmental of birds before."

"They remind me of a basketball team, these tall-necked guys strutting around in a pack saying, 'Look at us! Aren't we cool!' "

"Yeah, but you heard Diego. The poor guys are powerless. The females do all the choosing."

Everybody else was gone by then. I knew; I checked. I took a deep breath.

"But what if the female doesn't want any of these regular old guys? What if she wants somebody different?" I was going for it.

Noah shrugged. "Well then, I guess she has to go find the guy she wants. It's up to her."

I tried to take a deep breath, but I couldn't seem to get any air to go inside. "If it was up to me, I'd pick you," I said, my voice so low and shaky I didn't know if Noah could even understand me.

"What?" Noah was staring at me.

Did he think I was capable of saying that again? I turned away from his eyes, hoping I could say *something*.

"That thing I told you about Vincent was a lie. There's no Vincent. I mean, there is a Vincent, but he's just my neighbor, not my boyfriend. I'm his confidante. He tells me about all the other girls he goes out with and basically makes me feel lousy, but I'm not in love with Vincent and I never have been."

Noah came to life and moved up behind me. "Why did you tell me you were then?"

Why had I started this confession? "Because . . . because I didn't want you to . . . because I was afraid you'd think, you'd see . . . how much I liked you." The end of the sentence was almost swallowed up by humiliation. How could I have sunk so low as to say something like this to a boy? And now I'd ruined what I *did* have with Noah, a nice friendship, even if it would be over in a few more days. I wanted to run, but where could I go to get away? Back to the Albatrosses?

Oh my god, he put his hands on my shoulders and turned me around.

"Hey," he said seriously. "If it was up to me, I'd pick you too."

And then I got my first kiss. It was definitely worth the wait.

15/Noah

People just don't *say* things like that to each other. And I'm not going only on my own experience now. I've talked to plenty of guys about stuff like this — even a few girls. People just don't tell you straight out like that: "If it was up to me, I'd pick you."

Cat's an amazing person. And at the risk of sounding related to my newly deranged half brother, I have to say I've never felt like this before.

After I kissed her, we put our arms around each other. Not that sort of lazy embrace like you're dancing, but a real hug, like our insides wanted to be as close as our outsides. I mean, I've made out with girls plenty of times; I've even removed a piece of clothing or two, but I've never ever felt as close to another person as I did right then hugging Cat.

I don't know how long it lasted; I know I felt like I never wanted it to end, but finally you start to feel silly. I mean, what were the kiss and the hug saying, and what were we supposed to do next?

Cat looked up and smiled at me as we broke apart. She still looked a little embarrassed and I knew I ought to say something. As far as confessing feelings went, she'd done the heavy lifting so far; I'd only had to agree. But what was there to say?

Yes, I felt very close to her; I liked her a lot. But it was really kind of pointless, wasn't it? I mean, sure, we could spend a few more days kissing, but that would only make us want more from each other, and since that was going to be impossible, why get our hopes up? I was going to feel bad enough going back to the mess in Brookline without adding more heartbreak to it.

What could I say to her; what could I promise her? Nothing. Still, her dark eyes looked right inside me, and I couldn't turn away. We followed the trail to the beach with our arms wrapped around each other's waists.

Of course the minute Henry saw us he applauded, alerting the rest of the Albatross herd. He didn't say anything, though; he just smiled at us kind of sadly. I'll tell you, I hardly recognized the guy.

And of course the rest of this mature group had to give us thumbs-up signs and these patronizing little aren't-they-cute grins.

Cat was embarrassed too, and we separated to strip down to our swimming suits. The beach here was the nicest one so far, in a protected cove, the sand fine and white as flour.

I was not particularly happy to see Jeremy come running toward us, sopping wet and carrying a handful of seaweed. I'd taken pity on the kid at first because his parents seemed like such jerks, but I was just as glad when those Fogarty people took over the responsibility.

"Where were you? Look what I got!" Jeremy screamed, thrusting the smelly seaweed in my face.

"Great."

"There's lots of it out there. I'm gonna make a castle and put seaweed on the top for a roof!"

"Good idea."

Jeremy calmed down, then gave me a disgusted look. But the gaze he turned on Cat was even worse, the look you get when you find some food you don't like to begin with covered with green fuzz in the back of the refrigerator.

"How come you hang around with her so much? Is she your girlfriend or something?"

How did people *stand* to have little kids around all the time? Cat stowed her shorts and T-shirt under a bush and ran down to the water so I wouldn't have to think up an answer while she was listening. Why are you so perfect? I thought, as I watched her run to the water unself-consciously, as though she didn't realize how great she looked.

"Sort of," I said to Jeremy, knowing that wouldn't satisfy him.

"She can't be *sort of* your girlfriend. Either she is or she isn't."

"Well, you're wrong. She is and she isn't. She is for a few more days, but she isn't because I won't see her again after that."

"Why not? Couldn't you visit her?"

"It's not that easy. You want me to help you make a sandcastle?" I'd have to devote my life to this kid now to keep him from totally embarrassing me.

"Okay. But I don't see why you'd want a girlfriend anyway. Boys are more fun. Girls just holler at you, or else they want you to kiss 'em."

I had to laugh. "You could be onto something there, Jeremy. The thing is, when you get older, you won't mind the kissing so much."

Jeremy pretended to stick his finger down his throat.

Cat and I stayed away from each other that afternoon. I think we were both kind of shaken by whatever had happened in the morning. I could bring back the feeling of her hug just by thinking about it, and the more I stayed away from her, the more I thought about it.

When you liked a girl first and then it turned into something more, it was hard to figure out if the friendship was still the same. It was the friendship that made me like Cat in the first place, but now that things seemed to have gone further, I didn't know how to act around her.

At dinnertime we smiled at each other warmly and took seats a room apart. Henry took me in hand.

"Noah, don't screw things up. She's a winner. I know what I'm talking about."

"Since when? This morning you didn't know which end was up."

"You're not me. You *should* fall in love with somebody . . ."

"*I* should? I'm only sixteen! How come I should and you don't have to?"

Henry poured enough coffee down his esophagus to

142

drown himself again. "Maybe I'd like to fall in love," he whispered angrily. "Maybe I don't know how. But you do. Don't run away from it!"

I'd never seen Henry look so upset. "Henry, I don't think it's a matter of knowing *how*. You just do it."

Henry sighed and stared over at the table where Miyoko was sitting. Her two friends seemed to be lecturing her while she sat with her head bowed.

"Something stops me," he said quietly. "I never realized it before. I always made excuses: I liked to play the field, I didn't want to get caught. But that was all a crock. I built a wall around myself. The truth is, I was too damn scared to stick with one person."

"Scared of what?"

Henry shrugged. "Letting somebody see who I really am, I guess."

Miyoko was looking up now, stealing a glance at Henry. "I think Miyoko already knows who you are," I said.

Henry nodded. "Maybe. And the same goes for Cat and you."

"The difference being, I wasn't hiding."

Henry smiled. "Bro, we're Dad's boys. We learned hiding from the master."

I knew there was some truth to what Henry was saying. I was that way with people, too — only letting them get so far, then pulling back. I told myself it just meant I was a private person; I didn't need to go around spilling my guts to everybody. But I knew that wall Henry was talking about. You didn't just lock other people out; you locked yourself in.

"Who am I to give you advice, huh?" Henry laughed.

"Hey, can love be any more painful than feeling like this? I don't think so." He stood up and stretched. "Man, I feel like I'm ready for the glue factory tonight."

Before he could make a move, Miyoko was standing behind him. "We talk a minute, Henry?"

Henry took her hand and led her out of the dining room. It was amazing what Miyoko and a brush with death had done to Henry. He was suddenly somebody who thought about things, who could talk about things you wouldn't discuss in a locker room; he was a grown-up.

But I wasn't. And all this talk about love was too confusing. I had enough problems in my life without another one to complicate matters.

Diego stood up and made an announcement to the assembled diners. "If I could have your attention, please. As you know, the boat is moving toward our next destination: Isabela Island. We should arrive at our anchorage in a few hours. Tomorrow will be a long, tiring day, as we'll be hiking all the way to Volcan Alcedo and will need to carry packs with water and supplies. We will hike out again before dark, but the trip is strenuous, so I urge you all to go light on the liquid refreshment tonight and get to bed early." Everyone laughed politely, though Diego was even more fidgety than usual.

I decided I might as well take Diego's advice and get to bed early. Cat must have done the same thing. I didn't see her around anywhere.

But of course it was hard to fall asleep. It's not every day you have a thing like this happen. I kept thinking about what Henry said. There was part of me that really wanted to take that wall down. I also had the feeling that another kiss or two, a few more of those bear hugs, and the gates would open whether I was ready or not.

I must have finally fallen asleep. It was late, probably the middle of the night, when I heard the banging at the cabin door. I thought at first it was Henry because he wasn't in bed. Could he be with Miyoko? I wondered.

"Noah, wake up!" The door handle rattled. I let Cat in.

She was trembling, and for a minute I thought I knew why she'd come. And I was thrilled.

But then the words poured out of her. "He's taking them off the boat! Right now! He's stealing the tortoises! Help me!"

16/Cat

I couldn't sleep, what with everything that had happened. There had been a wonderful moment with Noah when everything was perfect, but as soon as it was over, things started to go wrong. First Henry and the others teasing us and then Jeremy with his stupid questions — I could tell Noah didn't like it. He didn't want people thinking I was his girlfriend.

It was just what I was afraid would happen. Now he wouldn't even talk to me; we couldn't even be friends anymore. I lay in bed thinking, why did I have to push things? At least I'd be able to spend the next few days with Noah, instead of missing him before he'd even left.

When I heard the engines of the boat cut back, I figured we must be at our anchorage near Isabela Island. Now I wouldn't have the gentle rocking of the boat to lull me to sleep. Lying there, twisting myself up in the sheets, I remembered Diego nervously telling everyone to get to bed early so we'd be rested for the hike in the morning. What was funny about that? His voice was shaky, kind of like the evening Noah and I overheard him telling Sofia to go to the party without him because he had too much work to do. He was . . . lying.

A chill passed through my body. What if he wanted everybody in bed early so he could get the tortoises off the boat? It made sense. He'd have to get rid of them before Friday when the celebration was supposed to take place on Casanova Island. He must be meeting someone on Isabela, someone he'd sell the tortoises to!

I got dressed fast and sneaked up to the rear of the second floor deck. This was the place I wished I'd spied from last time; you could see more from here. I crawled up to the edge like an iguana on a rock and peeked over. There were several pangas tied to the back of the boat, but no one in sight.

I *had* to be right about this, so I waited. Half an hour must have passed and I was starting to get cold lying on the deck. Just when I thought I couldn't stay there another minute, I heard a noise. It was a kind of puffing noise, heavy breathing. Another minute and there was Diego passing under the light, carrying a large tortoise. Bingo!

I watched as he struggled to get it in the panga by himself. Once his foot slipped on the stairs and I thought he'd drop the tortoise in the water, or maybe fall in

146

himself. He stopped then and hung onto the tortoise and the stair railing for dear life, swore, and then said something that sounded like a prayer. He managed to get that tortoise in the panga, and, after a deep breath, started back inside for another one.

There was only one thing I could do. Noah had said he was in this with me — now he could prove it. I slithered backward until I was away from the side of the boat, then ran to Noah's cabin.

He, of course, had been asleep. *He* wasn't losing any dream-time over one kiss and a little hug. He was so sleepy it took me a while to make him understand what was going on. Then he got dressed. I didn't go outside to wait for him this time; I stood and watched him pull on his jeans, put on a sweatshirt, and wished I was allowed to touch him just once more.

"You saw him put one of the tortoises in the panga?" he asked, careful not to look directly at me.

"Yes! Hurry up or we'll miss the whole thing!"

"It's not a movie, Cat. It's going to take him a while to haul four big turtles onto a little boat." He sounded mad at me. I didn't have time to figure it out.

We ran along the deck until we got close to the back of the boat. "Drop down!" I commanded, and Noah did, without an argument. We crawled to the edge; there beneath us was a panga loaded with three tortoises. Diego must have been going to get the fourth.

"God! It *is* the orphan tortoises!" he whispered.

I stared at him. "I told you! I thought you said you believed me?"

"I did! It's just that actually *seeing* them is different."

I heard Diego coming again and elbowed Noah to be

quiet. We lay there there side by side, just barely touching, while Diego struggled down the stairway with the final tortoise. Horrifying as the whole scene was, I couldn't quite forget how close I was to Noah. If I stretched out my arm I could put it around him. Not that I'd be *that* stupid again.

Diego finally got the last tortoise onto the panga and picked up two oars from inside the rubber boat. He began to paddle the craft away from the *Santiago*.

"Can't turn on the engine," I said. "He'd wake up the whole boat."

"Let's go get the captain!" Noah said.

I grabbed Noah's sweatshirt as he started to rise.

"No! What's *he* going to do? Besides, this is *our* adventure." The tortoise mystery was the only thing that belonged to Noah and me alone. Now he wanted to bring that silly captain in on it!

"Cat, this is not an adventure. The guy is a thief. We've got to do something."

"I don't want to wake the captain. Why don't we just take another panga and follow Diego? Then, when we see where he's going, we'll come back and wake people up."

Now Noah was staring at me. "Are you crazy? We should take a panga and follow him?"

I jumped up and made a run for the stairs. "Come on! If we don't hurry, we'll lose sight of him."

Noah followed me. "We can't do it! We don't know where he's going!"

"Probably to Isabela Island. It's right in front of us. We'll just make sure, then come back. How hard could it be? I thought you said you knew about boats."

"I do know about boats. But you don't even know how to swim!"

This did stop me for a second. "I'll just wear a life jacket, like I always do. We're not going that far, Noah!"

"We're not going anywhere, Cat!"

We glared at each other. "Fine," I said. "I'll go by myself." I took a life jacket from the stack and started down the stairs to the panga dock. I must confess I don't know what I would have done if Noah hadn't followed me, because I don't know one end of an oar from the other. I was calling his bluff. After all, it was *our* adventure; surely he wouldn't let me down on this. Surely we could have at least one adventure.

At the bottom of the stairs, I struggled to untie the knotted rope that held the panga to the *Santiago*.

I heard Noah behind me. "If I were you, I'd get in the panga before I untied the rope."

I jumped in the panga and Noah followed, sliding the rope easily out of its knot. I sat on the rubber edge like I would have in the daytime, but Noah motioned to me to get down inside the boat. "It's too unbalanced. Sit inside." He busied himself pulling on a life jacket and getting the oars into the locks, then finally he looked up at me, frowning.

"You know you're a crazy person, don't you? This is a totally insane thing to be doing. So why am I doing it?" He shook his head and began pulling on the oars. Miraculously, the panga moved away from the *Santiago*, out to sea.

"I can just barely see Diego's boat," I said. "It's over there." As Noah steered around to the front of the *San-*

tiago, the ship's bright lights threw a weird greenish glow on the water. At least we could see a little bit.

"He's turning away from Isabela. He's not headed for Isabela."

"He must be. Maybe he's just going around the other side or something. Follow him."

"Yes, master."

It was a lot scarier to be out on a little panga at night than it was during the day, under a hot sun, with two drivers and a guide along. At night it was cold and windy and the water was dark. "What do you think is swimming in this water right now?" I said, looking over the side.

"Sharks," Noah said.

"Why are you being so mean? You didn't *have* to come."

"No. I could have let you get in this thing by yourself and start paddling around in circles."

I didn't point out to him that I probably would never even have gotten the rope untied without his help.

"I thought you'd *want* to come. Don't you want to see what's going on?"

"Not particularly. Do you know how much trouble we'll be in when we get back?"

"Not if we catch a criminal," I reasoned.

Noah was quiet for a minute, then he sighed and smiled. "Cat, you're impossible. Truly impossible."

"I like you too," I said. Sometimes I just can't keep my mouth shut.

"Slide up this way."

"Won't we unbalance the boat?"

"Nah, I just said that to be bossy."

I moved up close enough to slide my legs under his.

It was warmer sitting together but awkward facing each other, so we both looked out over the water.

"Is that him? I can barely see him now," I said.

"That's him, and he's definitely not going to Isabela."

"But what other islands are out here?"

Noah shook his head. "There might be some smaller ones that aren't on the map. Listen, Cat, I think we ought to go back. I think we're headed straight for open ocean, and I can barely see anything anymore."

It didn't seem as if we'd come that far, but when I turned to look back at the *Santiago*, it was off in the distance, like a white star surrounded by darkness. A fog had settled between us and the big ship; it made the *Santiago* seem like a mirage. Following Diego had been a game, a mystery, an adventure, but suddenly I realized how very dangerous this whole thing was.

"Go back, Noah. We're too far from the ship."

"Don't worry. I'll turn on the engine and we'll get back quickly. We'll have to wake everybody up anyway to tell them about Diego."

Noah stood up and pulled on the rope that started the engine. It made a whirring noise, but then stopped. "It's not catching. I hope there's gas in this thing." He pulled again. The engine didn't start.

As Noah tried to start the motor, the wind picked up. The waves got bigger and the panga began to toss around wildly. We seemed to be heading into Isabela Island after all, but we were not coming into a beach. I could just make out a rocky cliff ahead of us.

"Noah!" I screamed, pointing at the rocks.

"I can't get the engine started; I'll have to row!" He put all his weight into the oars and we did move a little out from the rocks, but I could see that he wouldn't have the strength to get us all the way back to the *Santiago* in such turbulent water.

When we were clear of the rocks, I yelled, "Rest a minute. We're okay."

"No, we're not okay, Cat. Zip up your life jacket!"

With trembling, wet fingers, I zipped my jacket, then crawled forward to zip Noah's for him. "Noah," I said, "I'm sorry I made you come."

For just a second he rested his head on my shoulder. "I guess it's obvious I'd follow you anywhere." If I hadn't been so scared, I'd have been really happy.

He sat up and started to row again, but he was tired. "Let me try for a while," I said.

"You won't be able to. It's too hard."

"Maybe we can do it together. I can help!"

He stopped for a minute. "Okay. Turn around and sit up here in front of me. Like this. Put your hands in back of mine. Pull in when I say to. Now, *pull!*"

I've never worked so hard in my life. We pulled like that for a long time, maybe half an hour, I don't know, but when we looked up, it seemed we were hardly any closer to the *Santiago* than before. All we managed to do was keep from crashing into the rocks.

Finally I sagged forward. My arms were numb, my legs were cramped, and I was freezing cold. "I can't, Noah! I can't do it anymore!"

I turned to look at him. He was exhausted, too. "We can't give up, Cat. Rest a minute. We'll get back."

Obviously it was an impossible dream, but right then I believed him. "I know," I said. His face was dripping wet and I had the feeling some of that salty water wasn't from the Pacific Ocean. He was using every drop of energy and willpower he had to keep the panga off the rocks.

Then, just as I put my hands back on the oars to pull again, I heard a shout from across the water: "Hang on! We're coming!"

And I realized that the humming noise that had been ringing in my ears for the past few minutes had been the whining engine of another panga.

17/Noah

I guess the people on the rescue boat were shouting at us, but I didn't even hear them. All I could think about was pulling on those oars. The rhythm of it had become part of me. Even when Cat stopped rowing and turned to put her arms around me, I couldn't understand what she was saying. I knew she was crying, but that only made me pull harder.

When the boat came alongside us I could hardly believe it. It was like I was dreaming it. I watched one of the men tie the two pangas together, and still I just sat there in shock. Finally, when I saw them help Cat climb from our boat into the other one, I came back to life. But when I tried to stand up, I couldn't. I seemed to be paralyzed, stuck in rowing position forever. Two guys had to lift me from one boat to the other.

They laid Cat and me on the bottom of the boat and

covered us with blankets and a tarp to keep the water off. But we were already so wet and cold we were shaking like crazy. We had our arms around each other, which was comforting, but as we began to relax, everything started to hurt and we were both moaning.

Never had I ever been so scared as I was on that boat. Not just because I could drown or drift out to sea — I've been on boats before when the sea was rough and we were in trouble — this time I was scared because Cat needed me and trusted me, and I was going to let her down. And I realized that, more than any other person I knew, my mother or my father or Henry or anybody, Cat was the one person I didn't want to disappoint.

George, the German guide, was part of the rescue team; it finally got through to me that he was talking to us.

". . . take a few more minutes to get back to the ship . . . the squall is almost over," he was saying. "We've been looking for half an hour, ever since the boy's parents woke us up. But we didn't look in this direction at first. We assumed that, for whatever reason, you'd gone to Isabela. You were so far out it's just lucky that the search light caught you."

None of it made sense. "Boy?" I asked. It was as much of a question as I could put together.

"The young boy. Apparently he saw you take the panga out. I don't know why he was up at that hour, or why his parents weren't keeping an eye on *him*, but you're lucky he saw you go. Otherwise . . ." He left the horrors of *otherwise* up to our imaginations.

Cat whispered, "Jeremy! It was Jeremy!" I nodded.

Now that we were safe and the *Santiago* was looming

154

closer, George allowed his anger a little more rein. "You two are in very much trouble. Never have I heard of anything like this, people taking pangas out in the middle of the night."

Cat pushed herself up on her elbow. "We were following Diego. We wanted to see where he was taking the tortoises," she tried to explain.

"Diego? What are you talking about?"

"Diego stole the orphan tortoises of Casanova Island," I contributed. That was the limit of my strength.

George was openmouthed at the story. "Who told you —"

"I saw him," Cat said. "He and Andre brought them on board at Santa Cruz and hid them in Diego's room. Tonight he took them off the *Santiago* and rowed off in a panga. We tried to follow, but . . ."

"If this is true!" George was beside himself. We pulled up to the *Santiago* and he had to help tie up the pangas and then drag our frozen bodies up the stairs to the deck, where a welcoming party was waiting.

"Gott im Himmel! You are safe!" said Captain Bolmeier as we stumbled on deck. "You will give me an explanation for this when you have dried and warmed yourselves. I have not awakened your relatives, hoping that we would have good news of your return before worrying them all to death."

George had hurried up behind us. "Captain, they have a very strange story to tell!"

We heard George relating our tale of Diego and the tortoises, but we were already being hurried off to our rooms by Dr. and Mr. McNuff, who'd been awakened by Jeremy and had stayed up to watch the drama unfold.

Dr. McNuff happily took charge of Cat, hurrying her down to her room to shower and change clothes. Her husband was tired of the whole thing already, but Jeremy was wired and he followed me to my cabin, his dad trailing behind us.

"Man, that was awesome when you took the boat and everything! I was up on the top deck — you didn't even see me. I wasn't gonna tell anybody, but then I got kind of scared when I couldn't see you anymore."

I was trying to take off my half-frozen clothes, but Mr. McNuff was leaning against the doorframe so the door was wide open, and Jeremy was dancing around on my feet.

"Listen, Jeremy, I just need to take a shower now, okay?" I said, looking at his father for help.

"Let's go back to bed, Jeremy," Mr. McNuff said sleepily.

"Wait a minute! So is it okay that I told?" Jeremy wanted to know.

"It's fine. As a matter of fact, if you hadn't told, we'd probably be dead by now." I decided to sit on the bed and remove my sopping wet shoes and socks. I could manage that much with an audience.

"Really?" Jeremy's eyes bugged out. "You mean I saved your life?"

"Yeah, you did. Thanks, pal." I held out my hand for a high-five and Jeremy smacked me about ten times, leaping in the air each time.

"Jeremy, let's go," his father said again.

"Man, I never saved anybody's life before!" he hollered.

I pulled my sweatshirt off. I was getting into that

shower even if the kid followed me. "Look, Jeremy, I'll see you tomorrow, okay? We'll talk about it then."

"Yeah! I better go tell my mom now!" Jeremy said. He took off down the hall, yelling "Mom!" at the top of his lungs, just to wake up those few fortunate people who hadn't already been awakened by all the racket. His father trooped along after him, shaking his head.

The hot water helped a lot. The muscles in my arms had almost locked up solid once I stopped rowing, but the hot water thawed me out some. I was so tired I could have fallen asleep standing up, but I didn't want to go to bed. I wanted to find Cat. I knew she'd be looking for me, too.

Sure enough, she was at my door before I had my shoes tied.

"Let's go see what's going on," she said.

And then, right in the doorway of the cabin, I put my arms around Cat and kissed her again, a real kiss this time, a kiss that unzipped the life jacket I'd been wearing under my skin. I wasn't pretending anymore, even though the truth of it scared me silly. I wanted Cat to know that, whether I knew her for five more days or five more years or fifty years, she was the first girl I ever loved.

We went back to the panga dock then, our arms wrapped tightly around each other. A few people were standing around looking grim, but the McNuffs managed to drag Jeremy off, whining and wheedling. The captain had radioed to the Darwin Research Station to ask about the orphan tortoises. At first the person in charge said that Andre hadn't reported any problem, so they were sure the tortoises were fine. But when Captain Bolmeier said they had reason to suspect that Andre was in on the tortoise heist, they sent somebody else to check, and sure enough, the orphans were gone.

The people from the Research Station were going to Andre's house to question him, and George had taken a panga and a crew back out to look for Diego.

"This does not remove all blame from you young people," Captain Bolmeier assured us. "If you knew there was a crime being committed, you should have reported it to the proper authorities. How did you think you would solve this by yourselves?"

We didn't have a good answer for that, so we just shrugged and looked stupid. I didn't think he'd go for the idea that we wanted to have an adventure.

Then Captain Bolmeier looked at me closely. "You're the brother of the one who almost drowned the other day!"

I admitted that I was.

"Never have I had a group who got into so much trouble!" he fumed. "You two should go to sleep." He waved us away.

We wanted to stay up on deck to see what happened, but, of course, we were dead tired, so we got our blankets and curled up on a deck chair, together this time, and despite all the talking around us, we were asleep in minutes.

The last thing I heard the captain say before I drifted off was, "Where could he be headed? The only island in that direction is Lorenzo!"

18/Cat

We were awakened by a high-speed stream of Spanish being aimed by a furious Sofia at a wet and miserable man I vaguely recognized as Diego. My high school Spanish couldn't decipher most of it, but I did catch a little. "Ay, por Diós!" she shouted. "Qué te pasa, idiota!" Which means something like "My god! What's the matter with you, you idiot!"

The sun had just popped over the horizon, and the early birders, already standing at the rail with their binoculars, were trying to figure out what all the shouting was about. I sincerely hoped my parents wouldn't make an appearance until I could vanish.

The problem was moving. As I tried to sit up, little rockets of pain went off in my arms and back. Noah woke up to my groaning.

I didn't know what to say to him. His kiss had meant so much to me, had seemed to say so much. It wiped out the horrors of the panga ride and every little disagreement that had come before. But what if he'd forgotten it, or changed his mind overnight? What if the meaning was all in my mind?

He sat up beside me, obviously also stiff and hurting, but he put his arm around my waist.

"Good morning," he said, pushing my hair out of my eyes. He gave me just a little kiss this time, but there was a promise in it. This time I knew for sure.

Meanwhile Captain Bolmeier was trying to shush Sofia. "Please, my dear, this is of no use." He looked around at the passengers and smiled, as though nothing unusual was going on. "We need to discuss this rationally. Why don't we go down to my cabin and hear what Diego has to say?"

So the whole group of us trooped downstairs: Diego, Captain Bolmeier, George, Sofia, Noah, and me. I don't think the Captain particularly wanted us there, but there was no way we were missing this confession.

The captain's room was a lot bigger than the passenger cabins. There were even chairs for people to sit down. Everyone did, except Diego, who was too wet to sit, and Sofia, who was too mad.

The captain spoke first. "Before you try to think up some ridiculous story, Diego, let me tell you that the Darwin Station has confirmed the disappearance of the four orphan tortoises, and these two young people saw you take them off this boat and row them off somewhere. As a matter of fact, they followed you in another panga, one without any gas in its engine, and they are fortunate they did not meet their death being dashed against Isabela's rocks. You might be grateful you don't have that on your conscience this morning too."

Diego put his head down on his hands. "Oh, no! Never did I think someone would see me, and certainly not follow me! What can I say?" He looked at Noah and me. "I feel terrible! You are all right?"

"We're okay," Noah said. "But where are the tur . . . tortoises?"

Diego nodded. "I owe you all an explanation. This whole thing began because I was embarrassed to tell the truth. It would have been a small thing if I'd told years ago, but Andre and I let it get too big." He sighed and leaned against the bathroom door.

"When I came to Galápagos four years ago I was hired by the Darwin Research Station. Andre also was new. Our job was to search some of the small islands to see if we could find any bones or other evidence of tortoise species which might have been overlooked by earlier teams. We didn't expect to find live turtles or eggs; they were all supposed to be extinct."

"We know all this," Sofia said impatiently "You found the eggs on Casanova and you brought them back and raised the tortoises. But now you steal them! Do these islands mean nothing to you?"

"I didn't steal them, Sofia. Let me tell it! I had come here from Quito and Andre from Guayaquil. We were unfamiliar with the islands at first. We had maps, of course, but the maps were incomplete and the smallest islands were not even shown. Casanova, for instance, was not on the map . . . and neither was Lorenzo."

"Well, of course not. Lorenzo is very small. No boats even stop there," the Captain said.

"Our boat did. Lorenzo Island is where Andre and I found the eggs of the orphan tortoises."

"What? Lorenzo? You said —" Captain Bolmeier, Sofia, and George were all talking at once. Diego put up his hands.

"Please, I'm telling you. We found the eggs on Lorenzo, but we thought we were on Casanova."

"Casanova is a hundred kilometers northwest, around Isabela," Sofia said.

"Yes, but we didn't know that then. As a matter of fact, it was a year before the two of us realized our mistake. Once we found the eggs, we didn't go out from the Station as much. Our job became caretakers of the orphans. Everyone made a big fuss about it — our pictures were put up, our names were known. The orphan tortoises of Casanova Island became famous and so did we.

"Then one day we were out in the boat again, we had a new map which had Casanova marked on it, we knew our way around better, and we realized the tortoises were not from Casanova, but from Lorenzo. We thought we would look too foolish going back and admitting our mistake. As though we didn't know one island from another."

"That is the most ridiculous thing I ever hear!" Sofia ranted. "You just say, 'Hey, we made a mistake.' That's all. Instead, what did you do? Steal the tortoises? Kill them? What?"

"Kill them! Diós Mió, Sofia, I would never *kill* them! We made a plan, Andre and I. He would stay to be in charge of the tortoises and I would transfer to a cruise ship, the *Santiago*. So that when the time came to return the tortoises to their correct island, we could transport them on the cruise ship. Captain, you know how important it is that each subspecies is returned to its own habitat. Otherwise, all the careful work to raise the tortoises is for nothing. You know what we tell the passengers: not a shell or a feather or a rock must be taken off the island or transported to another island. We couldn't take the tortoises back to the wrong island. It would be betraying them!"

"And all this lying was due to your embarrassment over a simple mistake?" Sofia asked. Her anger was still boiling.

"It got away from us, Sofia. At first we were embarrassed, then, as the tortoises became so important — with the big celebration planned and everything — we were afraid we might lose our jobs."

"As well you should!" she said, and turned to leave the captain's cabin.

"Sofia! Wait!"

"No! I take my work seriously. I will not be the friend of a liar and a thief!" She slammed out the door.

Diego sank back against the wall again.

The captain shook his head. "I've never heard a story like this in my life. It's too ridiculous to be a lie. Just tell me one thing: What were you going to do when the tortoises were discovered missing?"

"At first we didn't think too much about that. We thought between the two of us, maybe we could cover things up somehow. But when this celebration was planned with so many people involved, we got worried. There was no good solution, so we decided to just get the tortoises back to the right island and see what happened next."

"Well, you see what happened," Captain Bolmeier said. "You endangered more than just the lives of tortoises." He looked at us, while Diego stared pitifully at the floor.

"I am so sorry," he said.

"George, you can leave now. Get the rest of the crew ready for today's hike," the captain said.

"And you two. I'd like to have a word alone with Diego."

"You're not going to fire him, are you?" I said. "Because really the whole thing was my fault. I mean, if I hadn't gotten mixed up in it, the tortoises would have gotten back to their island and it would have all been okay."

"No, no. Certainly it is not your fault, Cat," Diego said. "I feel responsible for the two of you. If anything had happened to you . . ." He shook his head.

"Do you want me to talk to Sofia," I asked.

"Cat," Noah interrupted. "I don't think they want us involved here anymore."

"You won't change Sofia's mind," Diego said softly. "She is strong-willed. She will not speak to me again."

Captain Bolmeier cleared his throat. "Well, I don't intend to fire you. I'll let these two in on that much of my decision. You've been a valuable guide and I'd hate to lose you over such a mistake. You will, of course, receive some sort of punishment. Perhaps your young allies will allow us to discuss that privately."

"Sure," Noah said. "Sorry if we caused any trouble." He pulled me toward the door.

"Trouble!" the captain said as we closed the door behind us. "This cruise has been nothing *but* trouble."

"I *knew* he was all right," I said, once we were back outside. "Why didn't I trust my first impression?"

"I feel bad about it too," Noah said. "I wish we could help him."

"Well, why can't we?" I asked him.

"Cat, don't you think we're in enough trouble already?"

"But Noah," I explained, giving him a smile I knew he'd appreciate, "now we're just going to fix everything up!"

19/Noah

There was no way Cat and I were going on an eight-hour hike. After our nap on the deck we felt more tired and sore than before. We were hungry though, so we got some breakfast and figured out what to tell Cat's parents and Henry about why we couldn't trek all over Isabela today. Captain Bolmeier had decided not to tell the passengers about the event since it made him look like kind of a boob who didn't know what was going on on his own boat. And if *he* wasn't telling, we wouldn't either.

Cat went to tell her parents she thought she was coming down with a cold, which was probably true anyway after the wet, cold night we'd just spent, and I decided I'd allow Henry to draw his own conclusions from my partially true story.

"This is going to be a great hike, man," Henry said as he smeared his toast with guava jelly. He was forking the food in as fast as the waiter brought it around. "Why don't you come?"

"I'm really wiped out. I spent the night in a deck chair."

"How come?"

"Well, Cat and I were talking . . ." I shrugged. "You know how it is."

"Cat? You and Cat were up on deck together all night?" Henry howled his approval.

"And where were you last night?"

He grinned. "Sorting out my life."

"In Miyoko's room?"

"Yeah. But mostly we talked. Can you believe that?

Me, alone all night with a beautiful woman, talking?"

"So?"

"So . . . I don't know. I guess . . ." he stuttered, his grin spreading slowly across his face like an oil spill. "I guess I love her."

"You guess?"

"I do. Yeah, I guess I do. Man, this is so scary." He shook his head. "It's great though."

"I know."

"You do?"

We sat there grinning at each other like goofballs until Miyoko showed up and slid into the chair next to Henry.

"Here," Henry said, peering into her eyes and offering up his jellied toast. "I saved you a bite. You want some of my juice?"

"Best juice I ever taste," Miyoko whispered.

"I told you this trip would turn out great, didn't I?" Henry said. "Man, I didn't know *how* great!"

"Yes, you did, Henry." I got up. There's only so much you can stand to watch of grown people feeding each other.

Cat and I waved to the intrepid hikers as they boarded the pangas. Poor Diego must have been ready to drop with exhaustion, but he had to lead the Albatrosses up a volcano anyway.

Once everybody was gone, we had an awkward moment. I mean, we knew we were both going to bed. We were so tired we could hardly stand up anymore. And nobody would have been any wiser if we'd both gone to the same cabin and curled up together.

But it seemed like it would have been too much, and I think Cat felt the same way. We only had four days

left together. Obviously we couldn't crowd a whole re-
lationship into that amount of time. On the one hand, I
wanted to be with her every minute. On the other, I had
to get used to missing her. It seemed like we were already
practically drowning in emotions; adding sex was only
going to make everything more confusing.

I walked her to her cabin. "I'll come by and get you
for dinner," I said, then pulled her into a weak embrace.
We were just kind of hanging on to one another, reluctant
to part.

"Noah, you know the way your mother feels about
men? That they're all the same and you can't trust
them?"

Oh, why did my mother have to make an appearance
now, just when I felt so good? I thought of her, glaring
at me across the breakfast table, thinking unmentionable
thoughts.

"I just want to say she's wrong," Cat said, looking up
into my eyes. "She's mad at your father, but you're not
your father. I know you're not, because you're not the
same as anybody; you're the best. And I trust you
completely."

I hugged her tightly then. There was a huge lump in
my throat, so I didn't say anything. I felt like I'd just
gotten the only present I ever wanted. I hoped I was
telling her how I felt without words.

"Oh, Noah, why can't you come back to Oregon with
me?" Cat whispered.

"I wish I could. I really do."

"Maybe there's some way. Maybe you really could
come somehow!"

"Cat, I don't think this is something you can fix up."

"Noah! Don't give up so easily!" Cat said vehemently.

I had to smile. "Okay. I won't." I kissed her then and said good night.

But separating, even for a few hours, wasn't easy. We looked down at our hands, the fingers unwilling to slip from their braid. How were we going to be able to say goodbye for good in only four more days?

As I finally walked back to my own cabin, I thought how unfair it was that I'd met someone like Cat and then had so little time with her. But as I was stretching out under the thin blanket I thought: at least I *met* her, at least I realized how wonderful she is, at least she feels the same way about me. I fell asleep thinking of Cat's arms around me, her hair against my neck.

Cat woke me up, as usual. I don't think she needed all that much sleep.

"Dinner's not for another hour or more," I complained, happily pulling her down onto the bed for a kiss.

"Hmm. I know. But, Noah, I've got a plan."

I put the pillow over my head. "No, not another plan!"

"Actually, two plans."

"Cat! What now! Can't we just relax and have a good time for the next four days?"

Saying the number out loud was kind of forbidden; I knew it was. Cat's face clouded up. "But, the more things we do, the longer the time will seem. And . . . the more memories we'll have . . . later."

I sat up and put my arm around her waist. "Okay. Tell me Plan A."

"Let's go. I'll tell you while we're on our way to the captain's."

We found the captain in the lounge before Cat had

time to give me all the details, so I let her explain her idea. Not that I could have stopped her.

Captain Bolmeier's shoulders seemed to droop when he saw us coming, but he led us to a table in the corner anyway.

"Captain," she began, a big, sweet smile on her face, "about the celebration we were supposed to have on Friday when the orphan tortoises were returned to Casanova Island . . ."

"Well, obviously the celebration's been cancelled," the captain said. "The people at the Darwin Station are rather upset about it too. Speeches had been written and a local baker was already starting to make a large tortoise cake for the occasion."

"So everyone wanted the celebration to take place?"

"Of course. Even I'm a bit disappointed. It would have been a break from the usual routine, going to a new island and so forth."

"Well then, why don't we have the celebration anyway?" Cat said brightly.

The captain stared at her as though her elevator didn't go all the way to the top floor. "My dear, the tortoises are *already* back on an island, have you forgotten?"

"Well, that doesn't matter, does it? They're back on the *right* island. I mean, you were planning the celebration and everything, but the tortoises would have gone to the wrong island! I think it would be good for everyone's morale if the celebration took place anyway, on Lorenzo Island. We could do it Friday, just like it was originally planned."

"Hold the celebration *now?*"

"You said it was already planned! What difference does

it make which island it's on? And it seems only fair that Noah and I would get to be in on it. I mean, if it wasn't for us —"

"If it wasn't for you, I wouldn't have so many gray hairs!" The captain picked up his glass and drained it dry, then slapped it on the table. He stared at Cat for a moment, then moved his gaze over to me.

"She's a tough one," he said, trying not to smile.

"I know," I agreed.

"I suppose it wouldn't hurt to call the Station and see what they think."

"Yes! You're not such a bad guy after all!" Cat said.

Captain Bolmeier frowned and shook his head. "Thank you so much." He stood up.

"Can you tell us one more thing?" Cat persisted. "What's Diego's punishment?"

"Don't worry. It's not so bad. He and Andre will not receive an increase in pay this year. It's a small price to pay for lying, but everyone understood that they had the best interests of the tortoises in mind or they would not have done it."

As the captain walked away, Cat shouted, "Let us know about the celebration!" He didn't answer, but shook his head, amazed.

"He's going to do it!" I said.

"Look, here comes Plan B," Cat said, pointing to Sofia, who was hurrying out of the kitchen with a bowl in her hands. "Sofia!" Cat called, running after her.

"What!" Sofia barked, turning so quickly soup splashed out of her bowl. "Aiyiyi! I burn myself!" She glared at us.

I had a feeling I knew what Plan B entailed, but it looked hopeless.

Even Cat was a little cowed by Sofia. "I . . . we wondered . . . could we talk to you a minute?"

"No. I'm tired. I'm having soup and going to bed." Sofia began to walk off again.

"Cat," I said, "I don't think this will work."

"It will!"

"Well, maybe you ought to do it alone. Woman to woman. I don't know what to say to her."

"Noah, I *need* you!" Cat begged. I doubted that was true, but who could turn down a plea like that? We chased after Sofia.

"Sofia! Wait! This won't take long, really. We feel responsible for what happened yesterday and we just want to talk about it a minute." Sofia, I thought, you might as well give up because Cat will bother you the rest of the trip if you don't.

Sofia must have realized this. She sighed. "Come down to my room. I give you five minutes, then I go to bed."

Sofia's room was only a little bigger than ours, and I wondered how she could live month after month in this tiny place. Cat and I perched on one bed while she sat on the other, sipping the hot soup.

"Diego said — " Cat began.

"Ahh! If you came only to talk about Diego, you might as well leave! I have wasted too much time on him already!"

"But why are you so mad at him? He made a mistake, but he was only trying to do what was best for the tortoises."

Sofia made a clicking sound in her cheek and continued to eat.

"Even Captain Bolmeier isn't really mad anymore," I put in. As long as I was there, I felt like I ought to help a little. "They might even have the celebration on Lorenzo Island!"

"What? Diego will have a celebration! The pig. He doesn't deserve." She threw her spoon into the half-empty bowl and tossed it on her desk.

"But I don't understand why you can't forgive him if everyone else does," Cat persisted.

"Because he lied to me," Sofia said. "More than once. How can I ever believe what he says again? No, no, no."

I couldn't help thinking of Dad when she said that. How long had he been lying to Mom while he was seeing somebody else? Surely he had loved Mom once. I knew he had! And if he loved her once, what happened that he didn't love her now?

And the scariest thought: Now that I loved Cat, would I *always* love her, or would it just go away, like the day after you've had the flu and you wake up and you know it had a terrible grip on your whole body just the day before, but now you can hardly remember what it felt like? I never wanted to forget Cat.

"But Sofia," Cat was saying quietly, "Diego only lied to protect the tortoises."

Sofia shook her head roughly. "He lied so he wouldn't look like a fool."

"But it wasn't such a terrible mistake. Can't you forgive him?" Cat pleaded.

Sofia was quiet a moment. "How can I trust him, now,

172

after this? If he told me . . . something else, how could I believe?"

"You can. Because I can always tell a good person when I see one. And Diego is good."

Sofia laughed at that and looked at me. "Is this true? Your girlfriend can see these things?"

Cat blushed a little, being called my girlfriend, and I wanted her to know the title was all right with me. "Yes, it's true. My girlfriend is something else."

20/Cat

While the people at the Darwin Research Station were finishing up the preparations for the celebration, the *Santiago* sailed to Rabida Island, which Noah and I enjoyed thoroughly. The sand on Rabida was an adobe-red color and the beach was strewn with sea lions that looked like they'd washed up on shore all at the same time, the way seaweed does. We took pictures of each other sitting in the midst of piles of these beautiful brown creatures, and I taught Noah as much about looking through a camera lens as he wanted to know.

Henry took some pictures of Noah and me together, which I know I'll be glad to have later, but at the time I would happily have fed Henry to the pelicans. He kept pestering us to let him take a shot of us kissing, but I refused. Hey, I'm new at this. I don't want it captured on film.

Noah and I made a pact not to talk about how much time we had left, and to just have as much fun as we could for the rest of the trip. And even though I don't think either of us ever really forgot that time was short, it made every hour, everything we did and said, that much more important than if we'd had years stretching out in front of us.

Diego was pleased about the celebration and called Noah and me aside to thank us.

"I hear you talked El Capitan into going ahead with the plans," he said. "I appreciate that. Almost the worst part of the whole thing was that everyone felt so cheated out of the celebration. This will be fun." He still didn't look all that happy, however.

"Is Sofia talking to you again?" I asked hopefully.

Diego sighed. "When Sofia gets angry, it's very bad."

"Maybe she just needs more time to get over it," Noah suggested. Diego smiled a sad smile and ruffled Noah's hair like he was a little kid or something. It's so aggravating to be treated like a child when your sixteen!

This morning after breakfast all the pangas went in to Lorenzo Island. We had time to search the small island to see if we could find the four famous orphans before the boat from the Darwin Station showed up with its speechmakers. This would be followed by a celebratory lunch for everybody back on the *Santiago*, complete with a large green tortoise cake.

We'd only been on the island for about five minutes — half of us were still drying our feet from the wet landing — when we heard Tomoko and Sachiko shrieking. "We find the first tortoise! Come see!"

Sure enough. Just off the main path in the middle of

some high weeds was an orphan. Diego came running up quickly.

"Ay, Diós Mió! You look fine, mi amigo!" He crawled up to the tortoise on his knees and gently picked up one foot, then another, looking him over. Diego had worn his dress uniform for the occasion and now the knees were filthy, but I don't think he could have cared less.

One of the Dolphins, an Ecuadorian man, found the next tortoise, and within forty-five minutes all had been located and checked out by Diego, who was as happy as if he'd been reunited with his own children.

The Darwin Station boat arrived soon after, and numerous official-looking men strode around, nodding at everyone. Captain Bolmeier joined them, and Diego and Andre directed them all to the locations of their reptilian offspring. Meanwhile several pangas full of folding chairs were being delivered to the beach and a tarpaulin was being erected over a small podium.

When everything was in place, Captain Bolmeier called everyone to please come and sit down. The sun was scorching that small strip of beach, and we envied the speakers who got to sit under the canvas.

Captain Bolmeier spoke first, referring only briefly to the "mixup between the islands." He assured everyone that the orphan tortoises of Casanova Island were really the orphan tortoises of Lorenzo Island, and they were happily home at last.

Then he asked Diego and Andre to say a few words. You could tell they were embarrassed, but also pleased that they were getting their chance at fame even though they'd messed up. They explained again about finding the tortoise eggs and raising them at the Darwin Station, and how happy it made them to see the tortoises living free.

Then Captain Bolmeier introduced a string of people from the Darwin Station, all of whom had something nice to say about Diego and Andre, but all of whom took way too long to say it. We were boiling out there.

The last person to speak was Señor Romero, the director of the Darwin Station.

"After talking with Diego this morning," he said, "I would like to announce a staffing change. I have always wished that Diego would return to the Darwin Station as a researcher. Today he has agreed to do so."

Everybody applauded and hollered; it was obvious they all knew research was what Diego wanted to be doing, not guiding tourists around week after week. I looked around to find Sofia, to see what her reaction was. She was standing in the back practically behind some bushes, and at first she just stood frozen with her arms crossed in front of her, looking bullets at Diego. But as everybody else yelled their approval, I could see her begin to melt too. A little smile crossed her face.

Captain Bolmeier told us all to board the returning pangas for the trip back to the *Santiago* for the fiesta luncheon. But I took Noah's arm and whispered, "Wait a minute. I want to watch Sofia."

We sat on a rock, taking a very long time to remove our shoes, pretending interest in yet another iguana. People were shaking Diego's hand and congratulating him. Sofia waited until the crowd was gone, then motioned Diego over. Of course she wouldn't go to him!

Noah and I, shoes off by now, wandered nearer so we

could eavesdrop. Noah was getting much better at sleuthing.

"Congratulations," Sofia said, almost forcing the word out of her mouth. "I know you always want to return to the Research Station." She held out her hand.

Diego took hers in both of his. "Sofia, I hope you can forive me sometime. Since you came to the *Santiago* you have been my closest friend. I have missed you."

Sofia softened a little. "And I you. But now you will be on the *Santiago* no longer."

"Perhaps you will come to see me when the boat docks in Puerto Ayora?" Diego asked tentatively.

"Perhaps I will." The slightest grin appeared on her face.

They were uncomfortable. Another minute and they'd be running off in opposite directions.

"Would you mind if I took a picture of the two of you together?" I asked innocently, popping out from behind the Palo Santo tree we'd been leaning on. Sofia rolled her eyes and clicked her tongue, but then Diego laughed and she laughed with him. So I took a few pictures of them; they even put their arms around each other (once I suggested it).

There's one picture where they're squatting down next to one of the orphan tortoises — I took it from down low so their faces kind of loom up over the tortoises's shell. I'm getting really good at this.

Back on the *Santiago* Noah and I ate lots of green cake — we even fed each other a piece, which I know is disgusting if you watch other people do it, but fun if it's you.

We spent the rest of the afternoon sitting on the beach talking while everybody else was swimming. It seemed like we needed to learn all the details about each other while there was still time.

I told Noah about Benson River, how it was warm enough to start your garden in February, and how by April the valley was full of pear and apple blossoms. How my house was on the outskirts of town in the foothills of the Siskiyou Mountains, and how my best friend owned horses we rode on mountain trails.

Noah said Brookline was mostly big houses and expensive shops. He liked going into Boston, but his favorite place to go was Maine. The shores were rocky and there were lots of little islands you could sail to. He told me he was worried that he might lose Maine because of his parents' divorce.

We talked about all kinds of things, silly and scary and sad. We wanted to say everything and know everything. I didn't say I loved him. I could have said it; it wouldn't have been hard, but I had a feeling it might scare Noah. He's not used to saying things straight out. If he could say he loved me, I would happily say it too, but I know he can't. It's all right; I feel it anyway.

Before going back to the *Santiago*, Noah made me get in the water for my first swimming lesson. He said if he could learn photography, I could learn to swim. I wasn't so sure. I hated the feeling of water getting in my nose. But then I loved the feeling of Noah holding me up as I floated on my back. I could look up into his smiling face surrounded by sun.

And another day was over. Tomorrow we go to Fernandina and see the only penguins that don't live at the

South Pole. And one more day . . . but I'm not counting.

I mean, look how much can happen in two weeks! I used to be a girl from Benson River, Oregon, who had one hopeless crush on one creep in sixteen kissless years. Who would have thought a trip to the Galápagos Islands would change my life? That I'd meet a boy with a snotty-sounding, hyphenated last name who lived in Brooklyn, but not New York. And that I'd fall in love.

Life's a funny thing. I like it.

21/Noah

Cat and I sat together on the plane as far as Quito. The only other time I've seen Cat that quiet was the first evening when we sat at her table on the *Santiago*. I misunderstood it for shyness then; now I saw that it was just thinking time, her brain making adjustments to new circumstances. We held hands. I kept looking down at our fingers so tightly woven. I just couldn't *believe* that in a few more hours we wouldn't be together anymore. Cat had gotten inside me somehow, and yet, soon we'd be thousands of miles apart.

Henry was in mourning already. Miyoko and her friends had gotten off in Guayaquil to catch a plane from there back to Japan. I could hear Henry, who was sitting behind me, sighing long and loud. Once he even groaned. I tried to think of something comforting to say, but I felt too lousy myself to comfort anybody else.

As Henry sat forward he pulled on the back of my seat. "Noah!" he said urgently into my ear. I turned around.

"What?"

"I'm going to ask her to marry me!" His eyes shone brightly.

"You are?"

"I'm going to call her tomorrow. When she gets home."

"Well, Henry, I mean, you've only known her for two weeks!"

"You've only known Cat for two weeks!"

"Yeah, but we're not getting married!"

"I bet you would if you were older, if you weren't just sixteen!"

Cat looked at me, surprised, and blushed. Maybe I would. I couldn't imagine ever meeting anybody I felt happier with. Still . . . marriage . . . the word made me shiver.

"But Henry, you're only twenty-two," I argued. "Look what happened to Dad's first marriage when he was young."

"Right. And look what happened to his second marriage and his third marriage, when he wasn't very young at all. Noah, we've got to stop comparing ourselves to Dad. We're not *him*. Just because he made certain mistakes doesn't mean we'll make the same ones."

"I know that!" I said hotly.

"I don't think you do. You thought Dad was perfect and then all of a sudden it turned out he wasn't. And now you think you have to be perfect, to show him how it's done, or something. But you aren't going to do every-

thing right either, kiddo. It doesn't work that way!"
Henry let go of my seat and I bounced forward.

It's funny. I never gave Henry credit for much except
being able to ski a terrific slalom, but he was not skim-
ming over the crust now. He was telling me the truth,
and I suddenly recognized it.

And then I didn't need to hate Dad any more, or
be so angry at him. He made some mistakes, that
was all. If there was one thing I learned on this trip
it was that people made mistakes. If they were lucky,
they could make amends, or at least do as little damage
as possible.

Maybe Dad fell in love too easily, but I knew now
how powerful that emotion was, how difficult to deny.
I thought someday I might even be able to forgive him
for hurting Mom and me. And I figured Mom would
eventually forgive me for being male, even if she never
pardoned Dad.

I leaned over and kissed Cat. "So, what do you think
about Chicago?" This was a continuation of the conversation we'd been having for twenty-four hours.

"Well, it sounds like a plan, Mr. Barker-Lowell," she
said, trying for humor.

"Yesterday you thought two years was too far ahead
to be planning. You had some California college on your
mind," I teased gently.

"That was yesterday. That was when I still had time
left." She sounded like she had a golf ball stuck in her
throat.

"Damn it, I'm not going to cry," she said, jerking her
hand away from mine to swipe at her face.

I pulled her over to me so that her head rested on my

shoulder. "Think about Chicago. There's Northwestern University, University of Chicago, University of Illinois at Chicago Circle — I'm sure there's even more than that. We'll find out about every single college in the Midwest. And if those don't work out, then you pick the place you want to go and just tell me. I mean it. It doesn't have to be half-way. My dad's paying — I'll make him send me out to California if that's where you want to go to college. I will!"

"Oh, Noah, I don't care about two years from now. I miss you this minute!"

Cat had a way of heading right into the truth that took my breath away. I unhooked her seat belt and pulled her onto my lap where I could hold her tightly.

I had decided this morning that I wouldn't be able to say the words, the ones we never spoke out loud in my family. The ones I was afraid I could never say. But now with Cat nestled into my shoulder and the inevitable separation close at hand, I felt it tearing at my chest, the words, at last, ready to go.

"Cat," I whispered. "You know . . . you know . . ." They were right there!

Cat sat up a little and let me look deep into her sorrowful eyes. "What?"

"You know I love you." When the words finally came they burst like a river through a dam. There was a sharp pain in my chest, as though something really had ripped open. "I really do love you, Cat."

"I know," she said, and kissed me sweetly. "I love you too, Noah."

We indulged in some serious kissing for a few minutes.

Finally Cat sat up, reached for her bag, and pulled out a wad of tissues.

"I'm not really crying," she said, dabbing at her face. She patted mine too. "Neither are you."

"Certainly not," I said, sniffing. "Don't you know men never cry?"

"I know. There was just a fire inside you, and your automatic sprinkler system went off."

"That was it, all right."

She sighed. "You know what else I'll miss tomorrow?"

"Besides me?"

She nodded. "The Galápagos Islands. It was so magical there. I mean, maybe if we'd met each other someplace else, we wouldn't have . . . fallen in love." I could have listened to her say that forever. It deserved another kiss.

"So you'll go back there for your honeymoon in ten years," Henry interrupted from the seat in back.

"Are you listening to us?" I complained.

"Of course I am. What else is there to keep me entertained? I'm in love, I'm alone, and I'm miserable."

"Plan your own wedding."

"I already did. Now I'm doing yours."

In ten years Cat and I would be twenty-six. Where would we be? *Who* would we be? Was there a chance we'd still be in love?

The plane landed before we were ready. But, of course, we never would have been ready. The Mancinis had to catch a plane for Dallas that left in an hour. Henry and I had a three-hour wait for a flight to Miami.

We stood in the middle of the concourse, our gate

183

number in one direction and Cat's in the other. Henry gave Cat a kiss on the cheek and a wink, then had enough sense to disappear for a few minutes.

Mr. and Mrs. Mancini shook my hand and said how nice it was to meet me and how nice that Cat had made a friend. I guess it's hard for parents to admit their children have grown-up feelings, even when the truth stares them in the face.

Cat wasn't crying anymore. She gave me a hug, one of her usual rib-crushing hugs and said, "Thank you, Noah. This was the best vacation of my life."

Over her shoulder I could see her parents smiling indulgently, probably thinking how cute we were, or something insulting like that. They were thinking *puppy love*, and it wasn't true.

I was afraid as soon as we parted, we'd both start thinking it had never happened. I wanted to say something she'd remember, something to think about when we had a whole continent between us, but what could I say to her in front of them?

I saw Henry picking out postcards at a booth across the way, probably already composing his proposal to Miyoko. He seemed to be holding up a postcard so I could see the picture on it. Two waved albatrosses, their soft, white heads leaning together.

What had Diego said about them? "These two mate for life. They may fly far across the world, but they will find this same small island again, and each other." I picked up Cat's hand.

"Don't forget our plan," I said. "Ten years from now we're going back to the Galápagos — together — for another two weeks in paradise!"